Murder at the

Church Picnic

A Mallory Beck

Cozy Culinary Caper (Book 1)

Denise Jaden

MURDER AT THE CHURCH PICNIC
First Edition. November, 2020.
ISBN: 979-8558315295

Join my mystery readers' newsletter today!

Sign up now, and you'll get access to a special epilogue to accompany this series—an exclusive bonus for newsletter subscribers. In addition, you'll be the first to hear about new releases and sales, and receive special excerpts and behind-the-scenes bonuses.

Visit the link below to sign up and receive your bonus epilogue:

https://www.subscribepage.com/mysterysignup

Murder has such a sting!

If anyone had told Mallory Beck she would become Honeysuckle Grove's next amateur sleuth, she would have thought they were ten walnuts short of a brownie. Her late husband had been the mystery novelist with a penchant for the suspicious. She was born for the muffin pan, not the binoculars, and yet here she was, having just solved her first murder case. It had all started with delivering a casserole to a grieving family and finished with the help of a sarcastic teenager, a cop with kind-hearted green eyes, and a cat with a hunch.

Maybe she should have thought twice about delivering another casserole. But this one was for the potluck at the annual church picnic, and what could possibly go wrong at a picnic?

Chapter One

ALMOST NINE MONTHS AND I still felt like a flake of eggshell in a bowl of yolks every time I attended a social gathering alone. At least today I'd made an extra effort to avoid any wardrobe malfunctions. Even if I did something brainless like leave the house without brushing my hair or putting on pants, I'd be meeting Amber, my new fifteen-year-old BFF, who, with any hope, wouldn't let me traipse through a public park in my underwear.

I collected the cheesy bacon and potato casserole from my kitchen and then said goodbye to Hunch, a cat with an attitude if I'd ever met one. He had recently broken his leg and dislocated his hip, so I was trying to have some grace for his bristly attitude. I compensated for his growls with my perkiest voice.

"I'll only be gone a couple of hours," I singsonged to him.

Cooper, my late husband and Hunch's true owner, used to talk to him aloud constantly. In fact, with Cooper, it had usually been less like talking to a cat and more like some kind of intelligent three-point discussion. I hadn't quite gotten comfortable with having conversations with my feline roommate yet, but then again, I didn't need his help in plotting my next mystery novel like Cooper had.

"Maybe I'll even bring Amber back with me," I told Hunch, and this earned me an uptick of his whiskers.

Amber had been visiting me almost every day since we'd solved the murder of her dad together and brought the guilty parties to justice. She always came around under the guise of a cooking lesson—I'd promised to teach her how to prepare everything from baked sourdough to ratatouille, and in fact, she'd assembled today's casserole pretty much on her own with only my instructions from the kitchen table. I'd simply popped it into the oven this morning to warm it up, filling my kitchen with the scents of savory sharp cheddar and apple-smoked bacon. Amber had wanted to make a casserole with bacon in it, and while I was as big of a fan of crispy pork as the next girl, we'd had to play around a little with the recipe so the salty flavor hadn't overpowered the rest. We'd started with nugget potatoes, but in the end, I'd suggested adding a couple of Yukon gold and Vitelotte purple potatoes to round out the flavors and add some vibrant color.

In truth, Amber probably did only show up for the cooking lessons. Me? I'd do almost anything for the company, and Hunch, I was fairly certain, would do almost anything to have someone other than me in his lair.

I left my cantankerous cat in my wake and headed for Cooper's Jeep with Amber's casserole in hand. After my husband's death, I'd driven his Jeep for months, trying to find the powerful feeling he'd claimed to have gotten from driving it, but today I chose it because of the FOR SALE sign posted prominently in the back window. I didn't often spend much of the daytime out in public, but today at the park would be the perfect opportunity to get lots of eyes on it. Surprisingly, posting the FOR SALE sign in the vehicle had made me feel the strongest

I had felt in the last eight and a half months since I lost my true strength—Cooper.

I took deep breaths to steady myself on my ten-minute drive to Bateman Park. I kept telling myself it shouldn't take this much bravery to simply leave my house. It would certainly have been easy—too easy—to back out on attending the annual church picnic if I hadn't made a commitment to Amber. She had originally asked me to go with her because she didn't think her mom would be up for it. As of last night, though, it turned out her mom wanted to go, and so that left me still feeling committed, but meeting her there instead of picking her up. I hoped these solo outings would eventually get easier with time and practice

I turned the corner onto Bateman Road and discovered my next problem. Finding parking might prove as difficult as interpreting my cat's growls. The picnic was supposed to start at eleven, in lieu of today's church service, and it was already five to. I didn't like to be late, especially with someone meeting me, but nevertheless, I turned the corner and drove farther from the park in search of a space big enough for this giant gas guzzler.

I should have expected as much on such a beautiful day, but most of the time, my brain still wasn't as quick on the uptake about normal life situations as it used to be. As I wove around various back streets, I passed plenty of people walking toward the park, arms loaded with lawn chairs, blankets, and food. I recognized one couple—Marv and Donna Mayberry—which only served to increase my already racing heart. Chatting with couples after losing your spouse felt a little like driving a three-wheeled car. Marv worked long hours, so it was more common to have one-on-one time with Donna, but apparently not today. Some people strolling toward the park wore dresses and suits, and I looked down at my peach T-shirt and denim capris, wondering if there was some kind of church picnic dress code I wasn't aware of.

At least Amber would be here somewhere, and I couldn't in my wildest dreams imagine her showing up to the park in a fancy dress. I'd yet to see her in something more formal than a hoodie and cut-offs. It was just a matter of finding her. Up the next block, I finally found a space big enough for the Jeep.

Cooper had kept a couple of lawn chairs in the back of his Jeep for as long as he'd owned it. They hadn't been used in over a year, but it was time to get the creaks out of at least one of them. I'd come back for the other if Amber hadn't brought her own. Thankfully, they had backpack straps on them, so I grabbed the red one on top and slung it onto my back. Then I reached for my purse, complete with suntan lotion and bug spray, and finally for the warm casserole. The scent of salty goodness wafted up toward me as I adjusted the lid. Now that it was fresh out of the oven, the flavors had baked into one another, the melted cheese had rounded it out, and it smelled amazing.

Foot traffic thickened as I strode closer toward Bateman Park, and I kept my eyes peeled for Amber and her mom. They both had auburn hair and were both striking in different ways—Amber with her big-eyed attitude and her mom with her bouffant hairstyle—so they shouldn't be hard to spot.

Before I could find them, I rounded a small hill to get into the park, and a flurry of activity captured my attention. Tables were being assembled with food under one of the two giant park shelters, kids chased each other around the playground, and at least a dozen carnival games were being erected between the food shelter and a big open field. I'd been happy when Amber told me our contribution to the day would be food because that sounded much more up my alley than setting up and manning a ring toss or a kiddie pool fishing pond.

I surveyed the nearly one hundred heads of those either helping set up or involved in clustered conversations, but Amber and her mom weren't among them. The giant shelter on my left consisted of a large wooden gazebo with a cement floor and a half dozen picnic tables under the overhang. The tables wouldn't have nearly enough seating for our congregation, but other church members busily set up oblong tables and chairs from the church basement all around the perimeter of the shelter.

The one other shelter in the park stood about fifty feet away, and this one had rows of white chairs lined up in front of the cement area and white tulle decorating the front rafters of the shelter. A nearby table overflowed with wrapped gifts. It looked like preparations for a wedding. Two men in suits straightened the twenty-or-so rows of chairs, and many of the formally-dressed folks I'd seen on the sidewalk milled around that side of the park. I let out a breath, glad I hadn't dressed inappropriately for the picnic after all.

As I headed for the church's picnic shelter where the hot food had been placed, a nearby commotion caught my eye. Pastor Jeff was in the midst of a hushed argument with a lady I didn't recognize. She couldn't have been more than five feet tall, but what she lacked in height, she made up for with her large pregnant belly, stretched tight under a pale pink dress.

She flapped her arms to the sides, and as I moved closer, I started to make out the problem. "The bride and groom expected to have the whole park to

14

themselves. It's their special day and they'll be here any minute! I'm their wedding planner. How do you think this is going to look for me?"

Pastor Jeff pushed his hands toward the ground and spoke in his usual calming and authoritative tone. "I understand your concern, Mrs. Winters, and I have no idea where the mix-up happened, but let's just take a deep breath and see what we can do." Pastor Jeff angled away from the pregnant lady, toward where the carnival games were being assembled. He quickly located his wife and called, "Emily? Let's try to keep all the games closer to the playground, all right?"

Between Pastor Jeff and his wife stood Marv and Donna Mayberry. They were one of the first couples Cooper and I had met at Honeysuckle Grove Community Church. Donna leaned into her husband and whispered something, likely an embellished rumor. And just like that, the giant game of telephone that always seemed to start with gossiping Donna Mayberry had begun.

"I don't care how much you move those games," the pregnant wedding planner said in an exasperated tone to Pastor Jeff. "The Bankses and the Albrights are still not going to appreciate kids running through their ceremony, and all the noise a church picnic will generate. They're not going to want these people they don't know hanging around their wedding!" She flapped her arms again. Pastor Jeff took a breath, about to speak, but she interrupted him. "Look, I don't know how the municipal office could think this park is big enough for both a wedding and a church picnic, but it's just not. I'm calling them right this second to sort this out."

I couldn't imagine the municipal office being open on a Sunday, but she pulled out a cell phone and marched away with it, not giving Pastor Jeff a chance to respond. That left our pastor staring straight at me, the only other person in the immediate vicinity. The deep grooves of his face told me he wanted to find a solution as much as the wedding planner did.

And like the last time I'd seen Pastor Jeff looking helpless, I wanted to do what I could to take that pained look off of his face.

"What can I do to help?" I asked.

Pastor Jeff wore a lavender dress shirt and khaki shorts that looked lovely together. I attributed his tidy and coordinated appearance to his wife, Emily, being here helping, instead of at her usual Sunday morning job in the church nursery. But in only one second, Pastor Jeff ran a hand through his sandy brown hair, and it stuck up in all directions, effectively ruining the put-together effect.

He shook his head. "I need to get the games moved as far away from the wedding as possible." He turned, and I took a step to follow him, but then he swung back around and said, "Actually, could you ask Sasha to gather some parents and corral the kids to keep them near the playground? That would help."

I looked to where he pointed to a lady in a long purple paisley dress. I knew the woman, or at least I had known her many years ago. She'd been my seventh-grade English teacher, back when I'd lived in Honeysuckle Grove, West Virginia, with my dad and sister more than fifteen years ago. Her hair had grown from shoulder-length to halfway down her back, and it was grayer than it had been back then, but she still clearly wore the same paisley dresses.

"You mean Ms. Mills?" I asked.

Pastor Jeff nodded, but he looked eager to rush off and speak with his secretary and the rest of the church staff to figure this out. "Yes. She takes care of our children's ministry."

If I'd had kids, perhaps I would have known that. Cooper and I had wanted kids, lots of them, but sadly, he'd been killed in a fire at one of the local banks shortly after we settled into town.

I nodded to Pastor Jeff, but still had my casserole dish in my hands, so I followed him toward his church secretary, near the food shelter, saying, "Yes, right away. I'll just put this down first."

Pastor Jeff was too concerned about his current problem to worry about me and spoke to his secretary from several feet away as he approached. "Did we not book both shelters for the picnic, Penny? Their wedding planner, Mrs. Winters, insists she has the park booked for a wedding today." He motioned to where Mrs. Winters stood angrily punching something into her phone's keyboard.

"Oh, I, um, I'm afraid I don't know." Penny Lismore was in her early twenties with bright naturally-orange hair and big blue naïve eyes. She had been the church secretary for a little less than a year. I only knew this because she had been new on the job when Cooper died, and she had made many apologies to me about not understanding procedures in booking a memorial service. Today she looked equally clueless as she picked at the side seam of her navy shorts. "Troy said he was going to book it."

I placed my casserole dish on a nearby table and looked up to where both Penny and Pastor Jeff had moved their gazes. Near the carnival games, with a clipboard in hand, stood Troy Offenbach, the treasurer of Honeysuckle Grove Community Church. He had trim blond hair, statuesque posture, and a stoic face that meant business, even at a picnic. My knowledge of Troy Offenbach was about as limited as my knowledge of Penny Lismore. He had printed off a detailed bill for Cooper's memorial service, and I had paid it.

Troy hadn't been particularly compassionate about the fact that I'd only just lost my husband a week prior, but I hadn't expected him to be. He was a numbers guy. If Cooper had taught me one thing from when I'd helped him research his mystery novels, it was that if you wanted to get a better handle on the cast of people surrounding your story, they could all quickly be reduced to certain stereotypes. Troy was all about the accounting, Penny was an employee who could follow simple instructions but wasn't much of a self-starter, and Pastor Jeff gave from the depths of such a big heart every time he came across a problem, no matter how large or small. I feared it might be the thing to break him.

"Troy!" Pastor Jeff held up an arm and beckoned his church treasurer toward him.

I took a breath and remembered the job I'd been given. Besides, did I really want to get in the middle of this situation with no easy answers? As I quick-stepped toward the kids' play park and my seventh-grade English teacher, the pregnant wedding planner moved back toward the trio of church workers looking exasperated.

"The municipal office is closed on Sundays..." was the last thing I heard as I strode away quickly.

Sasha Mills, the children's ministry coordinator, seemed no less frazzled. There had to be twenty-five kids under ten in her care, and her eyes darted from place to place as she called out short phrases such as, "Ethan, stop hitting her!" and "Amy and Zara, you're going to have to share!" and "Dominic, get down from there!" to the boy up high in the oak tree. Their parents, it seemed, were all busy helping with the picnic preparations.

"Excuse me? Ms. Mills?" I said, already feeling bad for interrupting this very busy lady. Ms. Mills had always been a bit of a softie, and if I were honest, it surprised me to see her still working with young children, ones I expected would know how to railroad over her instructions without a problem. After a couple of other called instructions, she turned to me.

"Yes?" She looked me up and down. Again, I doubted my capris and peach T-shirt. But when her gaze settled on my face, I suspected the look had more to do with a grown woman calling her Ms. Mills. It just seemed too strange to call my former teacher by her first name.

"I'm Mallory Beck—er, Vandewalker," I added, realizing she wouldn't know me by my married name. But I wanted to take up as little of her time as possible, as, out of the corner of my eye, I could tell that the little boy she'd called Ethan had started hitting the girl again. It wouldn't be long until screams ensued. "I'm not sure if you remember me..." I waved a hand. That part wasn't important. "Anyway, Pastor Jeff has come across quite an issue. Apparently, the park has been double-booked. He asked me to see if you could enlist the help of a few parents and corral the children into the playground area?"

As I said the words, Ms. Mills raised an eyebrow at me, and I realized that even if the consequences were a bomb that was about to go off or the impending end of the world, corralling this group of children was easier said than done.

"How can I help?" I asked, so at least she'd know she wasn't facing this problem on her own.

Ms. Mills took about three seconds to survey the situation, and then she pointed to a large red

Rubbermaid bin near the food shelter. "Why don't you get the bin of Nerf guns? I have an idea."

As I raced to grab the bin, Ms. Mills called out the names of a few nearby parents. They came right over, and she stepped onto the wood chips of the kids' playground area and called out, "Children, listen up! The grass and the trees are lava!"

There was maybe a one-second delay, and then all of the kids who were outside of the square of the wood-chipped area looked down at their feet and raced toward the playground as Ms. Mills called out, "Three, two, one!" She pointed the mothers who had joined her around the perimeter of the playground, and they spread out.

Kids pointed and laughed at the few stragglers who hadn't made it onto the wood chips in time, but I had to hand it to Ms. Mills. She had a much better grasp on how to handle these young kids than I would have.

Most of the church men and teens followed Pastor Jeff's directions and dragged tables and games away from the wedding shelter. Other than the young kids, nobody hesitated to pitch in and help.

The Nerf gun bin was heavy, so I dragged it behind me, but only a second later, it lightened. I looked over my shoulder. Amber Montrose had grabbed the other end.

"Thank goodness you're here!" I said, now much more glad about her presence as a helper than simply so I wouldn't be standing at a social gathering alone. "The park was double-booked with a wedding. Pastor Jeff is trying to figure it out and asked that we keep the kids corralled over here."

Amber smirked—her usual reaction to most problems. Today she wore a sleeveless black T-shirt with her cut-offs that read: BUT DID YOU DIE? Her auburn curls were held back with a matching black headband. It may have been her personal style of mourning, as her dad had died less than two weeks ago.

"That should be easy," she said sarcastically.

As we arrived at the playground, Ms. Mills was already in the midst of discussing "rules" for a new game with the kids. "Nerf guns are only to be used in the wood chip area," she said. "The grass is still lava, and if I catch you with a Nerf gun on the lava, you'll lose all weapons for the rest of the day. Got it?"

The kids barely listened. At seeing the bin, all twenty-five of them barreled toward Amber and me, and only a second later, the hoard had elbowed us away from the bin so they could get in closer. Nerf guns swung up and out of the bin, and I could immediately tell this could be another accident waiting to happen.

Ms. Mills joined Amber and me near the edge of the wood chips. "This isn't going to last long, but it was all I could think of on short notice. Can you find out what's happening from Pastor Jeff?" She turned to Amber. "Can you hang out on the far side of the playground and help keep them within the boundaries, Amber?"

Amber nodded and headed that direction. I wasn't sure if Amber knew Ms. Mills from children's church or if she'd also had her as a teacher at school, but I didn't have time to ask. I turned and raced back toward the food shelter.

More guests had arrived since I'd been focused on corralling the kids, and there was a stark difference between those who were clearly here for a church picnic—in shorts and T-shirts and carrying lawn furniture—and those in dresses and suits, here for a wedding celebration.

As I skirted around picnic-goers and wedding guests to get back to the pastor and his two assistants, the pregnant wedding planner shook her head at Troy and then strode away with fists balled at her sides. I followed her eye line to three limousines that had just pulled up to the curb of the parking lot.

As if there wasn't enough to stress about, apparently the bride and groom and their entourage had arrived.

Chapter Two

THE CHURCH STAFF QUICKLY formed a huddle.

"Penny hadn't organized the picnic before, so I stepped in to help," Troy Offenbach told Pastor Jeff. I was still a couple of feet away from them, but stopped in place, not knowing if I should interrupt.

"And you booked the entire park? Both shelters?" Pastor Jeff asked him.

Troy glanced away toward where the carnival games were now at a standstill of being set up without him there to direct the process. When he looked back to Pastor Jeff, he seemed almost out of breath as he said, "I'm sure I told them to book it the same as last year and every year before that. I don't know what went wrong, but I'll have to call the municipal office on Monday and sort this out. They'll have to give us a refund."

Pastor Jeff shook his head. "Monday is not good enough, and I'm not concerned about a refund. These people are getting married here *today!*"

"Right," Troy said, blinking fast a few times. "But it's a big park. We'll just keep to our side, and they can keep to theirs."

Even I knew that wasn't going to work. The two shelters were too close to one another. The hubbub of activity and current noise level only highlighted the fact that the bride and groom would need a pretty serious microphone system to overcome this cacophony.

And as if this thought was their cue, at that moment, the children with their Nerf guns decided the grass was no longer lava, chased one another outside of the square wood-chipped playground plot, and ran in figure eights around both shelters. A half dozen mothers chased and tried to discipline their children, but it seemed Nerf guns were akin to a shot of straight sugar to these kids.

"Ms. Mills doesn't know how she'll keep the kids corralled," I said needlessly to Pastor Jeff, simply to highlight the problem for Troy-the-treasurer's benefit. Even though it was ninety degrees out, he wore a yellow dress shirt and full-length slacks.

"She's going to have to, at least until the ceremony is over. Then I'm sure everyone will relax a little." Troy pushed his wire-rimmed glasses up his nose.

Before I had time to argue this, the pregnant wedding planner marched toward us with an entourage following behind her, including a very young-looking bride and the groom. I was surprised that not only was the groom allowed to see the bride before their wedding, but he was sticking so close to her, it almost seemed like they were attached by an invisible string. The wedding planner's light brown hair had come almost entirely loose from her ponytail. At least fifteen people trailed behind her, some clearly involved in the bridal party in pastel pink dresses and tuxes with pink bow ties, and others, I guessed by their ages, included the parents of the marrying couple. A photographer with a large camera hovered nearby, already taking photos.

But all I could focus on was the very beautiful—and very angry—bride.

Maybe just into her twenties, she wore a princess-style dress, with a ten-foot train that dragged on the grass behind her. She seemed unconcerned about dirtying her cream-colored satin as she dug her fists into her waist and glared at me, Pastor Jeff, and then pointedly at Troy Offenbach, as though Mrs. Winters had already informed her that this was all the church treasurer's fault.

"You'd better believe that *no one* is going to ruin my wedding day!"

One of her bridesmaids, a curvy girl in her late teens in a pale pink satin gown, moved up behind the bride to tidy her blonde cascading curls, which seemed perfectly in place to me. The photographer moved in closer and got a shot of the two girls before the bride reached back, annoyed, and swatted her bridesmaid away.

"Stop it! Do you think I care about my hair right now, Lacey?" The bride's high-pitched nasal voice made her seem a little less pretty.

The barely-twenty man in the tuxedo beside her grabbed for her hand. "Sweetie, let's figure this out. We could just move the ceremony over to the far end—"

The bride snapped her hand away. "We're not moving our wedding ceremony, David. In fact, I'm calling the cops!" She held out an open hand, and only a second later, her wedding planner placed a cell phone into it.

"Candi," the groom tried again, and I didn't know if that was her actual name or a pet name, but she just shook her head at him and continued to dial.

The photographer, as if doing his own part to break the tension, said, "Mr. and Mrs. Banks?" to a well-dressed couple in their late forties. "Can I just get a shot of you over by the flower garden?"

The woman held up an index finger to him and then turned to the bride. "Honey, this is your day. If everything's not perfect, we'll figure something else out."

"We will not figure something else out!" the bride practically exploded, but the older couple was already following the photographer toward a lovely patch of New England Aster and purple great laurel.

Pastor Jeff and Troy backed away. "We have to come up with a contingency plan. Maybe move things back to the church?" Pastor Jeff said in a hushed voice, so as not to be heard by the wedding party. "Or delay until next Sunday?"

Troy shook his head and furrowed his brow, the first sign I'd seen of him having any real emotion. "I don't think we can assign another Sunday to this. Do you know what we'd lose in offerings? And if we move the whole picnic at this point, how many people do you think would really come?" Troy crossed his arms over his chest, looking like a child that didn't want to do what he'd been told. "We have every right to be here, and I say

36

we're staying." He didn't wait for Pastor Jeff's argument. He swung around and marched for the carnival games, barking orders at all of those who had paused their setup duties before he was even close to them. "Let's get that ring toss up! The kids are getting bored..."

Pastor Jeff turned back to the wedding party group. Now that I looked them over, the three bridesmaids in satiny pink dresses and groomsmen in tuxedos stood out like royalty among the peasants. I pegged Mr. and Mrs. Banks, who were posing so naturally for the photographer near the flower bed that they could likely do it in their sleep, as the mother and father of the bride. The blonde lady wore a floral dress and looked very much like her angry cream-clad younger version. The father of the bride wore a tuxedo that appeared to have been perfectly tailored to his svelte frame. The bride was still ranting into a cell phone, pacing back and forth on the lawn nearby, with her groom less than a foot away, nibbling his lip and not doing a thing to help.

"See?" the wedding planner said to Pastor Jeff. "David and Candi are not going to stand for this."

So Candi *was* her real name. David, the groom, didn't seem nearly as motivated by this turn of events as his bride-to-be, and I thought he probably *would* stand for this, along with anything else that stood in his way.

As if he'd heard my thought, just then he said, "Oh, it'll still happen," loud enough that even I could hear him. "Candi will figure out a way to fix this." He followed Candi back and forth with his eyes as she paced, as if willing this statement into being.

As I surveyed the group of bridal party and family members standing around, listening to the altercation, in various stages of upset over the shared park, several things became apparent.

First, the bride's supporters and the groom's supporters were quite literally divided down the middle with a good three feet of lawn between them. Second, there was a noticeable class difference between the two groups. The bride, her bridesmaids, and her family all dressed as though they had money, made obvious by their designer dresses and suits, up-dos that could only be the result of a professional stylist, and an air about them as if they had all been severely displaced, even though they'd been standing here for less than five minutes.

The groom's side of the lawn, in contrast, while not as fancily dressed by a longshot, looked as though they were in no hurry to lend a hand or try and solve this predicament. They placed baskets and shopping bags of wedding supplies down at their feet, as though they suspected they would be standing here for quite some time waiting for the double-booking to get worked out. A few of them had already taken a seat on the grass.

The photographer returned and said, "Mr. and Mrs. Albright?" surveying the crowd as though he had no idea who they might be.

A shaggy-haired, fortysomething man in a slightly tattered navy suit that looked a couple of decades old and his wife in a loose-fitting beige dress raised their hands.

"Parents of the groom?" the photographer asked in confirmation. I didn't blame him. These two didn't look dressed for *any* wedding, certainly not their son's.

Mr. Albright picked up a huge oblong bag from at his feet. It was big enough to store a small person and filled with at least a dozen bottles of red wine in clear bottles, which stuck out at all angles. The stocky man didn't seem to struggle with the bag's weight as he moved with his wife toward the flower garden at the photographer's direction.

As they walked, I overheard the photographer say, "I'm from the Honeysuckle Grove Herald. I'd just like to get one quick shot of you folks if that's okay."

Wow, the local paper. I just assumed he had been a hired wedding photographer, but apparently, this union was newsworthy. I suspected the photographer was underplaying the process because he'd taken at least a dozen shots of the parents of the bride.

But I'd barely blinked, and sure enough, he was done with them. Mrs. Albright, with braids down either side of her head, wrung her hands, looking anxious as she made her way back to the gathering of people, while Mr. Albright took his bag filled with wine and sidled up near his son. I wondered if he'd gotten permission to uncork wine in a local park, or if perhaps it was non-alcoholic.

But my questions very quickly turned back to the other glaring questions of the day when Mr. Albright said, "Maybe it's not meant to happen today, son," to the groom.

David Albright visibly flinched away from his father and moved closer to Candi, who was still ranting into her cellphone.

David looked a lot like his mother as he started to wring his hands against one another. "Candi will get her way. You just wait."

Pastor Jeff had left my side to move over to where his wife had her attention divided between setting up carnival games and the bride on her cell phone. Penny Lismore, the church secretary, had also wandered off. That left me as the closest church representation with all of these wedding folks staring straight at me. I most definitely didn't want anyone to start challenging *me* to fix this, so I sidestepped a dozen feet away, probably looking like a klutzy showgirl, to find Amber near the playground.

"None of them will stay put," Amber said with a shrug, not looking nearly as exasperated about it as Ms. Mills or the other mothers clearly were. Kids had scattered around every corner of the wide-open park. Some chased each other with Nerf guns between the rows of white chairs set up for the wedding, even knocking a couple of the chairs over. I wondered if all this excitement was a result of the Nerf guns—a backfire on Ms. Mills' part, to say the least—or if someone had tried to bribe them back to the playground with candy. Two kids raced right in between Candi, the bride who had apparently finished her phone call, and Troy, the church treasurer, who in the last thirty seconds had erupted into a raging argument about who had more right to the park for the afternoon.

David remained nearby, watching the argument ping-pong back and forth, but didn't come to his bride's aid.

Candi waved her hands at the church treasurer, while her bridesmaid had reappeared behind her to tidy up her hair once again. The bridesmaid grinned from ear to ear, paying little attention to the hair she was tidying. I followed her gaze to where the photographer crouched nearby. The bridesmaid changed her angle and tilt of her head several times as the photographer clicked away on his camera.

As the bridesmaid turned to a new angle, Candi actually swatted the girl's hand away so hard I heard a smack. "I told you, I don't care about my hair right now, Lacey," she barked at the girl, oblivious to the photographer. "I let you into my wedding party. Isn't that enough for you? Now get out of my way!"

Lacey's face flushed as she pulled away from the bride, but then a second later, she squared her shoulders and marched toward the photographer. I sidled a little closer to hear her spelling her name for him—L-A-C-E-Y—while the photographer noted it. She followed it with her last name. B-A-N-K-S.

Candi and Lacey, I mused to myself. Now that I looked a little closer, I could see the sisterly resemblance. Candi was clearly older, but not by much. I couldn't help checking out her belly for half a second, but the satin bodice appeared smooth and flat.

Candi's parents stood nearby, involved in their own argument.

"Just go make sure Hector's behaving himself," Mrs. Banks told her husband. "All we need is him causing a problem after everything else today."

Maybe it wasn't so much an argument as an instruction because Candi's father simply nodded and started to obey, but not before Candi could turn from where she'd been talking a blue streak at Troy to add her two cents. "I told you this wasn't going to work with Uncle Hector here! Is this going to be a problem? Like I don't have enough to deal with today."

Candi scanned the park, and when her eyes settled, I followed her gaze to where a man near the church's food shelter, only a dozen feet from me, waved her off with a hand. He stood close enough to have heard her remark, and he looked straight in her direction, but he only started chuckling at it. Apparently, Uncle Hector had a sense of humor.

"Look, Hector," Candi's dad said as he made his way over. "Either stay in the white chairs or we're going to have to ask you to go."

"You're gonna send me away? Why don't you just take care of Ella? It's my niece's wedding day, for crying out loud!" he slurred and accented his words with a smirk. While the rest of the bride's family were dressed to the nines, this man wore jeans and a green plaid shirt. His eyes were glassy, like he'd been drinking even though it wasn't even noon.

"Nobody's sending you away. We just hoped you could stay in your seat for today, Hector." I could see why Candi's dad got pushed around by his wife. He didn't seem to have a commanding bone in his whole body.

"You just keep Ella in check." Hector pointed at the father of the bride, almost hitting him in the eye, then turned and stumbled toward the white chairs.

Mr. Banks moved back toward his wife, but my attention was rapt on Candi's Uncle Hector because as soon as Mr. Banks had moved away, he stopped in place and looked around conspiratorially. When helping research Cooper's mystery novels, he used to explain to me how little ticks, like darting eyes or excessive licking of lips, could often lead his main character, Marty Sims, to the guilty parties.

Hector didn't move toward the white chairs, as instructed, and something about his darting eyes told me he was just as guilty about something as a villain in a Cooper Beck novel. It seemed while all the adults from the church were either trying to corral their children, working on moving and setting up the games area, or following the argument between the bride and church treasurer with interest, the church's food shelter had been left unattended.

I pulled out my phone, pretending to take a photo of the chaos in the park, while I watched Hector out of my peripheral vision. He looked both ways and then quietly slipped under the church's food shelter. I glanced around to find Pastor Jeff or Emily, but they were dragging a games table out past the playground and were out of earshot.

When I turned back, Hector was closing the lid on a big blue Rubbermaid container stashed under one of the shelter's picnic tables.

He moved away quickly, and I felt unsure about confronting the drunk man, so instead, I raced forward toward the Rubbermaid container, wondering if it contained a float of money or some other valuable item. Uncle Hector appeared, of anyone on the bride's side, like he could use a few extra bucks. But I didn't get there because right at that moment, Candi let out the loudest shriek I'd ever heard.

As I looked over, she slapped at her shoulder, stumbled forward a few feet, and collapsed to the ground.

Both Troy and David swatted at the air around them as Candi's parents raced to her side.

"Oh, no! Was there a bee?" Candi's mom looked up at the groom and church treasurer from where she kneeled beside her daughter. Candi gripped her neck as though desperately gasping for air. Even from my distance away, I could see that her hands were covered in red hives.

David nodded. "She arched her back like she'd been stung between the shoulders." He looked around and called out loudly to no one in particular, "Does she have her EpiPen?"

Candi's dad bent and stroked his daughter's hair. "It's going to be okay, honey. You're going to be fine!"

Candi's eyes appeared glazed over, like she couldn't take in anything happening around her, including her dad's voice.

The wedding planner rushed over with a white sparkly handbag tight between her hands. "I have Candi's purse. Let me see if she packed an EpiPen." As she rooted through Candi's small bag, she called out, "Does anyone have an EpiPen?" Before anyone could volunteer one, she added, "Wait! I found it!"

Seconds later, she struggled to bend down around her big belly beside Candi on the ground, fumbling over the package. The wedding planner seemed skilled at many things, but bending to the ground wasn't her strong suit in her current state, and she clearly didn't have a clue how to use an EpiPen.

David stood by, dumbfounded, while Troy snatched the package from the wedding planner, bent at Candi's legs, pulled up her dress just enough to reveal a pink garter, and a second later jabbed one side of the tube into her thigh.

I turned my attention to Candi's face and waited for what felt like an eternity. Her eyes flickered and then closed, her hands fell from her neck, and seconds later, she lay perfectly still.

I moved out of the church's food shelter to get a closer look. Lacey Banks was jabbering away to the newspaper photographer nearby. "I don't have any allergies," she said as I passed. "I can't even imagine having an allergy to something like bees. I mean, you wouldn't even want to leave the house!"

Everyone surrounding the bride had clearly been through this before with her, and I was sure they knew what to look for. The setup for the church picnic had paused, and everyone stood watching from their own vantage point. It felt like the whole park was holding its breath.

I had no idea what to expect from a severe allergic reaction. How long did an EpiPen usually take to kick in? I figured I must be overreacting, and yet

I couldn't fight the feeling I should call for an ambulance.

I sidled back from the large circle that had gathered around Candi's still body and pulled out my phone. As the 911 operator answered and I relayed the information of where we were and what had happened, a police car pulled up along the curb behind the line of limousines.

Officer Alex Martinez stepped out, and I had never been so happy to see a familiar face.

Chapter Three

"I JUST CALLED 911," I told Alex as I rushed over to meet him just outside his police car.

"Because of a park rental dispute?" He raised an eyebrow like I'd lost my mind.

I shook my head, quickly putting together that he had arrived because of Candi's call, not due to my emergency call only seconds ago. Alex's eyebrows deepened into a furrow. I had known him in seventh grade when he'd been my number one crush, and I had learned way back then how to read his expressions. His green eyes darkened.

He had a way of looking angry when he was actually worried or confused.

"No, there was a wedding double-booked in the park and the bride collapsed. She was stung by a bee, and they've administered an EpiPen, but last I saw, she didn't seem to be responding."

We both looked across the grass to where the crowd surrounding Candi had grown considerably. Mr. Banks had his daughter hanging limply in his arms. He walked quickly toward the parking lot with Mrs. Banks on one side and David on the other.

Alex marched to meet him. As I kept pace, he asked me, "And you called 911? How long ago?"

I had to jog to keep up. "Not more than a couple of minutes."

"Sir," he called out to Mr. Banks, "there's an ambulance on route. I'm going to call in and see how far they are away, but I suggest you place her down and wait at the grass near the edge of the parking lot. If she still doesn't revive on her own, they can treat her on the way to the hospital."

"But the EpiPen always works!" Mrs. Banks said. The words came out so strong, they almost sounded as though she were blaming Alex for this.

"I understand." Alex nodded, and I was impressed at his aura of calm, even though I could tell by the way his fingers rubbed at the seam of his dark police pants that he was anything but. "Let me just check on the ambulance's arrival."

He hurried toward his police car, and Mr. Banks started to bend to place his daughter down, but neither of them got very far before the ambulance siren could be heard. Seconds later, it turned the corner onto Bateman and pulled alongside the first limousine.

Paramedics emerged from the two front doors, and Alex raced over to meet the first one. I couldn't hear him from where I stood, but by the speed of his lips, I could see he was relaying the situation to them efficiently while the paramedic opened the back door to the ambulance and removed a portable stretcher.

Mr. and Mrs. Banks spoke frantically to the other paramedic near the rear of the ambulance. Much of the crowd had followed the Banks family to the parking lot. The paramedics instructed Mr. Banks to place his daughter down on the stretcher, then proceeded to check her pulse, pupils, and blood pressure. I couldn't hear what was said between the two paramedics, but a seriousness filled the air as they loaded Candi into the back of the ambulance.

Alex moved away, holding up his hands to the growing crowd. "Folks, please move back from the parking lot so the ambulance can get moving as quickly as possible."

People listened, murmuring worriedly to each other. The back ambulance door closed with Candi, Mrs. Banks, and one of the paramedics inside, while Mr. Banks and David rushed toward the closest limousine.

Mere seconds later, both vehicles were gone. Others who must have been close to the family followed suit, quickly getting into vehicles and driving off in a hurry.

While I stood in place, stunned at everything that had just transpired, Pastor Jeff approached Alex. "Did they tell you anything, officer? Is she going to be okay?" Concern leaked out in Pastor Jeff's voice, and worry etched lines into his face.

The people around the park— both picnic-goers and wedding guests—were all at a standstill, their eyes squarely on Alex and Pastor Jeff. Even many of the kids had stopped racing around, understanding that something serious had happened.

"They were going to treat her on route to the hospital. Her family is with her," Alex said in way of comfort because there didn't seem to be too much else to be said. I watched Alex's eyes carefully to see if he held any expertise in this area or might have gotten any extra insight from the paramedic he spoke to, but he looked just as clueless as I was.

Pastor Jeff nodded at least ten times, his eyes steady on Alex, and I could see him trying to come up with anything that could make this situation better. Then he turned to face the church picnic side of the park. "Folks, I hate to do this, but I'm calling the church picnic for today. We'll talk about whether or not something can be done to reschedule, but under the circumstances, I feel this will be the only thing we, as a church, can do to help. If any of you would like to remain and join a prayer circle, I'd like to see us do what we can to support the wedding celebration that was planned to happen here today."

He seemed to be choosing his words carefully. I quickly scanned the crowd for Troy to see how angered he was at this new information, but I couldn't see him anywhere on either side of the park.

Pastor Jeff clapped his hands together, and that seemed to set all of the church-going folks into the motion of packing up.

When I turned back to Alex, he had his cell phone to his ear. I couldn't make out what he said quietly into his phone, but only a second later, he shoved it into his pocket and asked me, "Do you know the bride's name?"

"Candi. Candi Banks." As I spoke, Alex pulled out his notepad and scribbled some notes. "Her parents, Mr. and Mrs. Banks, went with her to the hospital, along with her groom, David..." I snapped my fingers, and the name came to me. "David Albright." I looked around for young David's hippie parents, but they were nowhere to be seen in the crowd. "Mr. and Mrs. Albright must have followed them to the hospital."

Alex nodded as he made notes. "Anyone else from the wedding group that might know the bride and her family well, from your estimation?"

I surveyed the wedding side of the park. Many people had moved into somber-looking groupings. Several of the white chairs had been rearranged haphazardly, and a few were occupied, but not in a way like they were waiting for a wedding, more like they were settling into a campsite for the weekend.

I spotted the pregnant wedding planner near the wedding shelter, arranging bouquets, probably at a loss of what else to do.

"It looks like the bride and groom's family, as well as the wedding party, have gone along to the hospital," I said, and then pointed. "That's the wedding planner. Mrs. Winters, I think her name is. I'm sure she could figure out who in the crowd is connected to the bride."

It had been difficult to tell how many were here for the wedding earlier when the park had been filled with a mix of well over a hundred picnic-goers and wedding attendees, but in the couple of minutes that I had been talking to Alex, it seemed many had either followed the family of the bride to the hospital or gathered their children and rushed them out of a scene of so much excitement. There was now a clear separation between the picnic-goers, who were busy packing up, and the wedding guests, who seemed to be waiting to be told what to do.

"I should probably help clean up." I looked from Ms. Mills, trying to connect kids with their parents, to where the meek pastor's wife was trying to organize packing up the games. Troy was still nowhere in sight.

Pastor Jeff stood near the food shelter, organizing a prayer circle, which already included almost a dozen people.

Alex nodded. "I have to check in with the station." He motioned to his police cruiser behind him, and then glanced at his notes. "But I'll check in with Mrs. Winters and find you before I go."

I nodded and headed off toward Ms. Mills. In truth, I was torn between joining the prayer group and staying nearby to see if I could help either Alex or Emily Hawthorne. Ms. Mills only had four kids under her care now, and two of them were the pastor's twin boys. She didn't need my help, but I headed there anyway, trying to push away my instincts to join the prayer circle. Candi Banks had been so unresponsive when they took her away, and I couldn't get the image out of my head.

It wasn't that I didn't believe in prayer, but I'd had a shaky relationship with God since Cooper died. I still didn't understand why He would have taken someone so young, so good. Amber and her mom had already joined the prayer group, and I wondered why I couldn't get past my nine-month-old tragedy to pray for another family if they could get past their much fresher one.

"What can I do to help?" I asked Ms. Mills.

She smiled, much more relaxed than she had been fifteen minutes ago. "I'm fine. Why don't you join the prayer circle?" She motioned in that direction.

I took in a breath and angled in that direction, but just then, Alex crossed from his cruiser, making a beeline for the wedding planner. His buckled forehead told me that something had changed in the last two minutes.

I intercepted him. "Is everything okay?"

He kept his eyes on the wedding planner, and his mouth formed a frown as he shook his head. "They couldn't revive Candi Banks."

"I—what?" Alex finally met my eyes, and I said the words so he wouldn't have to. "She's dead?"

One solid nod, and then Alex pushed on toward Mrs. Winters. I sucked in a breath and held it. Ever since Cooper's death, I couldn't watch people being given tragic news, even on TV. Plus, after so recently helping Amber through her dad's death and confronting a murderer, my first inclination was to protect myself and my new best friend. And so, finally, I headed for the prayer circle and nudged my way in beside Amber.

About twenty people had their heads bowed while Pastor Jeff continued praying for the bride's health, her family, and the various stresses of the day. He prayed that somehow the bride and groom could still have the wedding of their dreams.

I swallowed against my parched throat, knowing I should probably open my mouth and inform Pastor Jeff of the severity of the situation, but I just couldn't do it.

"What? No!" My thoughts were interrupted by a loud cry from across the park. I followed the sound to see Mrs. Winters with arms splayed open, a look of shock on her face. "She can't be dead! Candi can't be dead!"

Alex had a hand on her shoulder and was pushing his other one toward the ground, clearly trying to calm her down.

But she swatted his hands away and started pacing with her hands out. It looked like she was asking Alex questions, either that or murmuring to herself, but I couldn't hear anything else from my place across the park.

"I can't do this." The emotional words from close by snatched my attention. Mrs. Montrose shook her head at Amber. She had the same pasted-on smile as she'd worn at her husband's wake only a little over a week ago, but her quiet voice was shaky. "I have to get out of here."

Amber nodded, looking pretty shaken up herself, but ever the strong daughter, she took her mom's hand and led her out of the prayer circle. As she left my side, she murmured, "I'll call you later."

"Of course," I said. She was being the strength her mom needed, but who was being her strength? I hoped as I got stronger, I could be there for her more.

Pastor Jeff had been stunned a moment ago, but he quickly seemed to gather his wits about him. "Folks, listen up! The Banks family needs our prayers now more than ever."

Chapter Four

BY THE TIME I LOOKED up from praying, Alex had calmed down Mrs. Winters some, and most of the wedding décor had been packed up. Men in suits with somber faces hauled white chairs toward a large van in the parking lot, while Mrs. Winters stood nearby, dabbing at her eyes and talking into her phone.

The church games had been packed up as well, and the crowd had thinned considerably. Emily Hawthorne was packing up food supplies under the nearby shelter. I went to help.

"Several people forgot to take their dishes home," she said either to me or herself.

"That one's mine." I pointed to my white casserole dish with the orange and blue flower emblem on the side.

She sighed. "I guess I'll have to call around about the others."

"Why don't you let me do that?" I said. I glanced at two large coolers nearby. "If I can borrow those coolers, I can take all the food and dishes and return them to their owners. You and Pastor Jeff have enough to worry about."

Emily looked up at me with a sad smile. "Thank you, Mallory. I'd sure appreciate that."

I was surprised she remembered my name. We'd had a short conversation at Cooper's memorial service, but the community church had several hundred members and had hosted several memorial services since then. Plus, Emily Hawthorne was usually needed in the church nursery.

As I organized the remaining six casseroles to fit into the coolers, Emily instructed a couple of men from the church to move other supplies to her vehicle. When one of the men picked up a blue Rubbermaid container, it jarred my memory.

But it wasn't the same Rubbermaid container Hector had been digging into. That one, at twice the height of all of those left, seemed to have already been packed away and into a vehicle.

Emily was headed toward the parking lot with an armful of paper plates and cups, but I stopped her. "Hey, I know this isn't too important at the moment, but when you unpack the bins, if you find anything missing, let me know. I saw someone suspiciously digging into one of them earlier."

Emily paused and furrowed her brow. Then she nodded. "I'll let you know," she said before continuing her trek toward the parking lot.

Pastor Jeff and Emily probably erred on the side of being too trusting. Even if the church had brought a large float of money, and it had been absconded by Candi Banks's Uncle Hector, I doubted Emily Hawthorne would ever mention it again. Especially after everything that had happened today.

By the time I had retrieved my Jeep and loaded up the leftover food, it seemed almost everyone had cleared out of the park.

Another police car arrived and two officers got out on either side. One I recognized as Detective Reinhart, the handsome sandy-haired detective who had been willing to help Alex with Amber's dad's murder case, even though neither of them had been authorized to investigate. I had only seen Detective Reinhart from a distance before, but he reminded me of a Ken doll who was likely married to a beautiful Barbie. The other cop wasn't bad-looking either, and I had to wonder if the Honeysuckle Grove Police Department only hired the most attractive men in town. Although, I supposed that didn't hold true for the sixtysomething overweight and grumpy Captain Corbett.

The officer I didn't know headed for Pastor Jeff, who was chatting with a couple of the only church-goers still left at the park. The officer pulled him aside to speak with him, and the couple waved goodbye as they started to head for the parking lot, but the officer held up an index finger, and they remained in place a few feet away.

Alex stood near where the wedding setup had been, having a serious-looking conversation with Detective Reinhart. Alex held a roll of yellow crime scene tape, and Detective Reinhart took notes down in a notepad.

I hurried over toward them.

"Albright," Alex was telling Detective Reinhart. "A-L-B-R-I-G-H-T."

Detective Reinhart paused his notetaking, turned, and flashed an easy smile at me, as though they weren't in the midst of a life-and-death crisis. "What can we help you with, Mrs. Beck?" His voice was much deeper than I'd imagined it, and I felt a silly school-girl flutter at the fact that he had remembered my name. But thankfully, only a second later, my brain came back online, reminding me of why I'd really come over.

"Is there something wrong?" I looked down at the roll of crime scene tape and then over to the detective. It seemed like an odd question, as clearly a lot had gone wrong in the last hour. But this was a detective on the force. Why would he be here for a bee sting, even if it was fatal? Why would Alex have gotten the crime scene tape out now, after almost everyone had left?

And Detective Reinhart seemed to understand my true question. He nodded toward Alex. "Why don't you fill her in, ask her some more pointed questions, and get that tape up?"

As the detective strode away, Alex's gaze flitted away from me. He wasn't filling me in fast enough, so I pushed. "Alex, what's going on?"

When he looked back at me, his eyes were serious. "It wasn't a bee sting."

I blinked. Then blinked again. "What's that, now?"

He glanced at Detective Reinhart again. When he turned back to me, he said, "When they removed the stinger, it turned out to be a tiny needle, inserted into Candi Banks's rear shoulder, not a bee stinger. I need you to tell me everything you saw here at the park from the moment you arrived until now."

If I'd thought Pastor Jeff looked tired this morning, it was nothing compared to how he looked by the time the police had questioned him, his wife, and the rest of the people left at the park. I felt equally exhausted after rehashing the events of the morning and as the notion started to register with me that what happened to Candi Banks this morning hadn't been an accident. They wouldn't have further information until an autopsy had been performed, but they were clearly treating this as a murder investigation.

Pastor Jeff and his wife, Emily, trudged toward their car with the last of the church supplies. I said goodbye while Alex went over to compare notes with the two detectives. The main section of the park had been cordoned off with police tape, and a forensics team had arrived to comb over the place.

"Thank you again for taking the leftover food, Mallory," Emily said. She shook her head. "The Banks family is going to have a heart-wrenching time ahead of them. I wish there was a way to give them all our extra casseroles, so it could be one less thing for them to worry about."

It just occurred to me now that I hadn't seen any caterers at the wedding. But Mr. Albright had been carrying a fair bit of wine. Perhaps they'd just had a cocktail reception planned. I glanced over at Alex, an idea coming to me. When Detective Reinhart had come over to talk with Alex, I'd heard him ask Alex to run by the Bankses' house while he went to the hospital.

"You know...let me see if I can't make that happen," I said to Emily.

As soon as she left, I strode over to Alex just as he finished speaking with Detective Reinhart. The two detectives headed for their dark blue vehicle. Before I could so much as open my mouth, though, Alex turned a question on me. "Did you happen to see a man named Hector Banks here earlier? Mrs. Winters mentioned him, and we wanted to ask him a few questions."

Drunk Uncle Hector. I'd forgotten all about him when I had relayed my story to Alex. I nodded. "He was here earlier. I think he was the uncle of the bride. If I had to guess, I'd say he'd already had one too many Mai Tais for breakfast."

Alex raised an eyebrow at me. "He was drunk?"

I nodded again. "Candi and her mom had been quite vocal about not wanting him here. Candi's father walked away from where Candi and the church treasurer were arguing to talk to Hector, to make sure he wasn't going to cause a scene. Shortly after that, I'd seen him sneak into the church's bin of supplies. I'd meant to check on what he had been digging for, if there might have been a cash box or something, but only seconds after that, Candi was stung." As soon as I said the words, I recalled it hadn't truly been a bee sting that killed her. "Er...hurt."

Alex flinched on the word "sting" but made a note of everything I told him.

"I asked Emily to check and make sure nothing was missing from the bins, but she was pretty tired, so..."

Alex nodded. "That's okay. Steve Reinhart wants me to head over to the church and track down that treasurer after I go to the Bankses' house, so I'll look into it then."

"Detective Reinhart again, huh?" I asked. The last time Alex had helped in solving a murder, Amber's dad's murder, Detective Reinhart had gotten all of the credit for Alex's work, due to some bad history between Alex's dad and Police Captain Corbett. Alex had been trying for years to get promoted to detective, but seemed to get pushed down at every turn.

Alex nodded, eyeing me as though trying to read into my question. "He's letting me help out with some of the more peripheral interviews. If I can prove myself instrumental in solving this one, you never know what could happen."

I bit my tongue to hold in all my questions about what else they had discovered through their questioning, knowing Alex wouldn't be able to answer them, especially not here, where Detective Reinhart and his partner were still within view.

But now this gave me extra ammunition to ask the question I'd initially had for Alex. "The church pastor's wife, Emily Hawthorne, thought the extra food from the picnic might be helpful to the Banks family in this time of tragedy." I motioned to where the food had been set up earlier. "They're going to be going through an awful time, and it would be one less thing for them to think about. Do you think it would be okay if I followed you over there and offered it to them?"

Alex twisted his lips in thought. "Sure, follow me there, and if Mr. and Mrs. Banks have returned already, I'll ask them if they're interested. But they may just want to be left alone at this point, at least until Steve can get to them to ask a few questions. Steve's just sending me as a precaution in case they've left the hospital."

I nodded and strode back to my Jeep to follow him. But as I got in, started the engine, and then caught up to Alex's police cruiser, I wondered how I had volunteered myself once again to deliver food to a grieving family.

And had Candi's death truly been another murder?

Chapter Five

THE BANKS MANSION WAS no less impressive than the Montrose mansion—Amber's home, which I had seen when I'd helped solve the mystery behind her dad's murder. In fact, while the Montrose mansion included many sculpted shrubs and bushes around the property, as well as sturdy walnut furnishings, the Banks mansion looked more like a property from a movie set, with large white pillars near the front door and a giant fountain in the center of the roundabout driveway. It felt like the difference between old money and new money.

I had planned to wait in the Jeep until Alex called on me, but just sitting in my driver's seat in the roundabout driveway made me feel silly and on display, especially in this hot weather. Without taking the time to ask if it was all right, I followed Alex up the front steps from a few feet back, carrying the potato bacon casserole Amber had made. There was plenty more food in the Jeep, but I'd start with this one so I could be responsible for getting my own casserole dish back.

The doorbell let out a long, varied chime, and we waited in silence for someone to answer. When two voices sounded from within, but the door didn't open, even after a long wait, Alex reached for the bell and rang it again.

After a full minute, the wide white door in front of us swung open. I recognized the teen girl who answered immediately. She was almost as young as Amber, but her blonde hair, which had been curled and half tied back an hour ago, had now been straightened with a flat iron, and she wore a thick layer of eyeliner she hadn't worn earlier.

Lacey Banks, sister of the bride.

Instead of the pink bridesmaid dress, she had changed into a black mini dress that looked both too short and too tight for her frame as it buckled around her stomach.

"My parents are still at the hospital," she said in a bored voice before Alex could open his mouth, as if she'd just said the same thing to twenty other people. The girl forced a fake smile.

"Oh, I see." Alex pulled out a business card and passed it over. "Can you please have them call me as soon as they get in? I'm sure my partner has located them at the hospital, but just in case he missed them."

Lacey took the card, but shrugged noncommittedly.

"And you are...?" Alex asked. It was exactly what I would have started with if someone seemed unhelpful in a murder investigation. While Alex had interviewed me, I had told him about Lacey and the way Candi had snapped at her as she'd fixed her sister's hair. I hoped Alex had put together that this was the same person, but he had conducted several interviews and taken copious notes today.

I hadn't wanted to consider the possibility that Lacey could have killed her own sister, but looking at her detached attitude now, I had to assume she either hadn't heard about her sister's death yet, or she was responsible for it.

"Lacey. Lacey Banks," she said. I waited for her to spell it out like she had for the newspaper photographer, but she didn't bother for Alex.

"And you're Candi's sister?" Alex confirmed.

Lacey scrunched up her face as if it angered her to still be talking to him. "Yes, and if you want to talk to somebody about what happened, you should talk to Troy Offenbach. He was right there fighting with her like he always used to when it happened." She started to close the door, but Alex intercepted the movement with a hand on the door.

"Wait, are you saying she knew Mr. Offenbach?" I asked, something about this suddenly seeming too coincidental.

Lacey rolled her eyes and said, "Uh, yeah," in a way that might as well have been *duh*. "Back when she pretended she had some kind of halo."

I wanted to know more about this because had loud and angry Candi and the staunch church treasurer been a *couple*?

"And does a Mr. Hector Banks live here?" Alex tried to get a vantage point inside the house over her shoulder, but she crossed her arms and shifted into his view. "Or do you know where I might find him?"

"He doesn't live here." Again, she tried to close the door on us. This time I said something to stop her.

"I'm sorry about everything that happened at the park today," I said, purposely keeping it vague in the event that she hadn't heard the tragic news about her sister yet. "And we at the Honeysuckle Grove Community Church wanted to offer you some of the food from our picnic today, if it would be helpful." I held out the casserole in my hands.

In less than a second, I knew Lacey's answer. Her face screwed up so tight I thought she might get a cramp. "You want to leave your leftovers here?"

"No, I—they weren't even touched. We couldn't go ahead with the picnic, so..." I trailed off when she shut the door in our faces.

I followed behind Alex toward our vehicles, a bit stunned. "You're not going to ask her anything else?"

Alex shook his head as he reached for his door handle. "It's Steve's case. If he wants to handle the questioning in a certain way, that's up to him. I was only told to see if the parents or Hector Banks were here, and I don't want to get anything wrong."

I knew Alex had to follow protocol if he ever wanted to advance within the department, but it frustrated me to no end that he couldn't follow his gut and press this young girl for some answers.

"Do you know Troy Offenbach?" Alex asked me.

"Not really. He's the church treasurer," I said, even though I was quite certain Alex knew that much. "I didn't know he knew Candi, though. I mean, Candi acted like she blamed Troy for the double-booking right away, but I figured that was because her wedding planner had told her it had been the church treasurer's fault." I thought back to make sure this was true. "Strange, though, if they did know each other, and if they seemed to have had a contentious past, that they both booked the park on the same day. And on the day she died."

"Strange indeed," Alex said. A gleam ignited his green eyes. I got that familiar feeling like we were on a case together again. "I'm headed to the church next. Feel like following? I've been working Sundays for as long as I can remember, so you probably know the staff and members better than I do."

I wasn't sure about that, as I'd only been to church once since Cooper died, but if this was an invitation to help—not to mention find out more about what really happened this morning—I wasn't about to say no.

Chapter Six

ON THE DRIVE TO THE church, I pieced together the little bit of information I knew.

One. It sounded as though Candi's death was the result of a needle someone had purposely stuck into her back. I doubted it could have hit a nerve that killed her. Blood loss couldn't have been the cause, or there would have been a lot of blood on the grass where she'd collapsed. That led me to believe there'd been some kind of poison on the needle. A poison that acted like some kind of allergen, I thought, recalling the hives on her hands.

Two. Troy Offenbach had some kind of a contentious past with Candi, and they'd been arguing right before she died.

Three. There hadn't seemed to have been much love between the Banks sisters, and Lacey had been fiddling with Candi's hair shortly before she died.

Four. And while I had nothing concrete against Drunk Uncle Hector Banks, he was still on my radar if Mrs. Winters had mentioned him, and Alex had been instructed to track him down. I looked forward to finding what had been missing from the church supplies.

I'd always had a lot of respect for Cooper and his ability to piece together murder mystery novels, but maybe I wasn't so bad at it myself. Then again, Cooper always used to say, "It's never the most obvious culprit."

Besides, this was real life, not some carefully-crafted Cooper Beck novel.

On the drive over, I considered what we could ask Troy Offenbach. It seemed Alex might not be willing to ask him anything of consequence, but that didn't mean I had to keep quiet. Maybe I could help get Alex some pertinent answers and, without him, even breaking protocol.

First, I'd certainly ask him how long he'd known Candi Banks. Next, if he had known that Candi had planned to get married at Bateman Park today.

I had worried the church might be deserted on a Sunday afternoon, but as I pulled into the parking lot behind Alex, there were a couple of other cars in the lot. One was Pastor Jeff's silver sedan. I hoped the small green car belonged to Troy Offenbach.

As I walked alongside Alex from the church parking lot, I listed off my theories. When I got to Lacey Banks' name, I reminded him, "Candi snapped at Lacey several times right before she collapsed because Lacey had been trying to fix Candi's hair. Candi was angry and acted really disrespectful toward her sister. Plus, why isn't she at the hospital? Do you think her parents have even told her about Candi's death yet?"

Alex twisted his lips as he thought this over. "Fixed her hair from the back?" he finally asked. I nodded. "And you said the two of them weren't getting along very well?"

I shook my head. "Even if you can't conduct the interview, you can deliver all the relevant information to Detective Reinhart before he goes there himself."

"You're right." Alex nodded and nudged my shoulder in what I thought was a thank-you. "I can definitely do that."

Unfortunately, Troy Offenbach wasn't at the church. When we asked for him in the church office, Penny Lismore told us, "I think he went home for the day. He was quite upset about everything that happened at the park."

I glanced at Alex. I supposed any of us could have been so upset by being in close proximity to such a huge commotion that we'd want to take the rest of the day at home, but it certainly seemed to confirm what I'd taken from Lacey's comments: Troy and Candi had some kind of significant history.

Penny was busy sorting through the carnival game pieces and not at her desk, but *she* didn't seem rattled enough to go home for the day. I looked around for the blue bins, but they hadn't been brought into the office. "Do you happen to know if Troy knew the bride, Candi Banks, from before today at the park?" I asked.

Penny shrugged. Her usual bubbly personality had dissolved in the last couple of hours. "I can't say Troy and I have ever had much in the way of personal conversations."

Alex asked, "Can I please get a contact phone number and address for Troy Offenbach?"

Penny looked up at Alex, and her mouth formed an O for a brief second, as if she hadn't noticed his police uniform until just this second. "Um, of course, officer," she said.

Penny hurried to her desk a few feet away and jiggled her computer mouse to bring her screen to life. A few seconds later, she had scrawled a phone number and address onto a sticky note. She passed it across the front counter to Alex.

"And is your pastor in?" Alex asked. I had no idea what he planned to ask Pastor Jeff that the detectives hadn't already asked him, but I was just glad he had let me tag along this far. I could already tell this would be one of those situations where I wouldn't be able to think of anything else until we had some answers about what actually happened to Candi Banks.

"He's somewhere in the building." Penny pointed out the office door and toward the worship center. "The twins are here, and last I saw, Sasha was watching them, but you might find them all down near the children's ministry wing."

I'd never ventured down to where the children's ministries took place, but I said, "Come on, I'll show you the way," and led in the direction of the worship center as though I had. "What do you want to ask Pastor Jeff?" I murmured to Alex as we made our way through the giant church lobby. The high ceilings made it feel as though we should be extra quiet.

Alex shrugged. "I got the impression Penny doesn't know Troy well. I figured the pastor probably knows him at least a little better."

That made sense.

At the outside doors to the church lobby, a dozen blue Rubbermaid bins had been stacked. I pointed. "These must be the supplies from the church picnic." Alex headed straight for them, clearly understanding that I was referring to Uncle Hector's covert pilfering. "It was a big blue bin," I added.

Most of the blue bins were only a foot in height. All the taller bins were a light gray—except for one. Alex headed straight for that one and pulled off the three light gray ones that had been stacked on top.

Alex pulled a pair of blue latex gloves from his pocket and slid them on before lifting off the Rubbermaid's lid. He didn't have to dig far before uncovering what Uncle Hector must have been digging for. Or come to think of it, he probably hadn't been digging to *find* anything. More likely, he'd been digging to *stash* something. Alex pulled out a quarter-full bottle of whiskey and held it up for me to see.

"I doubt the church staff brought that along," I said with a raised eyebrow.

Alex nodded. "I'll double-check with Pastor Jeff and then pass this along to Detective Reinhart."

On top of one of the Rubbermaid bins, I saw a roll of black garbage bags. I grabbed one and offered it to Alex, motioning to the bottle.

He smiled with one side of his mouth, the way that always reminded me of my seventh-grade crush. "You don't think I should barrel in there with a half-full bottle of whiskey, spouting questions?"

I suppressed my own smile. "I don't think it would be your best tactic, Detective Martinez." It was a title he hadn't been given yet, but he'd earned it as far as I was concerned.

He seemed to appreciate my confidence, but said, "Actually, I'm going to take the whole bin as evidence. They may want to fingerprint it."

He followed me toward the children's ministry wing. As I opened the glass door at the far end of the lobby, I knew I had the right place. Boyish laughter echoed down the hallway. I followed the sounds and told Alex, "Jeff and Emily have twin boys. I think they're six or seven."

We rounded the corner into a wide-open playroom. Bright red bins of toys lined the edges of the room. Ms. Mills and Emily sat on kiddie chairs in the middle of the room, a can of disinfectant wipes between them on a table and the bin of Nerf guns in front of them. One by one, they were wiping down all of the guns—or at least all of the guns not in the hands of Jeff and Emily's twin boys.

The boys had a gun in each hand. They ducked behind standing easels and chalkboards so they could peek around and shoot at each other.

Pastor Jeff was nowhere in sight, but Emily and Ms. Mills were talking in hushed tones about "the awful situation" and "what the family must be going through," and so my best guess was that they were rehashing everything that had happened at the park.

"Any idea where Pastor Jeff is?" I asked. Alex placed the blue bin down, just inside the room.

Emily and Ms. Mills looked up at us. Emily did a once-over of Alex's uniform and stood quickly. "I can go find him."

"It's not urgent," Alex told her, as her voice seemed to hold some sudden tension. "I'd just like to have a word before I leave."

Emily hurried out of the room, no less anxious. Ms. Mills continued cleaning the Nerf guns, and I figured the least I could do was help while we waited. I took a seat in Emily's warm kiddie chair and helped myself to a disinfectant wipe. "How long have you worked for the church?" I asked Ms. Mills as I picked up my first Nerf gun and started wiping.

"Oh, I just volunteer," she said. "Only for the last few months, since Mrs. Latham moved away."

"Mrs. Latham used to run the children's ministry?" I confirmed. Ms. Mills nodded. "So you probably don't know our church treasurer very well."

"Troy? No, not really. It's a big church and I don't usually come in during the week. I'm getting to know everyone in the congregation with kids, though. One day they'll likely be in my class, if they haven't been already, but I don't think Troy has a family yet."

I nodded. Troy did look a little young to have a family. One of the Hawthorne twins peeked around an easel just then and fired a Nerf bullet right at Alex's chest. He slapped a hand at it melodramatically, let out an "Owww," started to fall, and then at the last second swiped up his own Nerf gun from the floor and fired back. I bit back a smile at seeing the little kid in him.

Alex and the twins were still chasing each other around the big open room and shooting at one another when Emily returned with Pastor Jeff. He cleared his throat, taking everyone's attention except for the twins, who easily ignored their dad and kept playing, no matter how somber his countenance today.

"Oh, Pastor Jeff. Yes." Alex straightened his short-sleeve black police shirt, trying to match the pastor's serious nature. "I stopped by to speak with Troy Offenbach, but I understand he's gone home for the day?"

Pastor Jeff nodded, and when he looked at the floor, his head turned to a shake, as though remembering all that had transpired that afternoon. "He was quite shaken up after the ambulance left the park."

"Oh, he left straight from the park? He didn't come back here?" Alex asked. Pastor Jeff shook his head. "Did he know Candi Banks?"

Pastor Jeff's head snapped up. "Not that I'm aware of. Why?"

"We heard their discussion at the park became heated quickly." Alex tapped a finger on the edge of the Nerf gun in his hand. I suspected he was nervous, either because of interviewing a church pastor or because he had found himself helping in a possible murder investigation. Maybe both.

Pastor Jeff nodded, running a hand through his already messy hair. "She was very upset when she arrived and saw our church congregation scattered across the lawn. Plus, Troy tends to get defensive when he feels any blame has turned on him." Sadness and regret leaked out in the pastor's every word.

"Candi's sister, Lacey Banks, indicated that Candi and Troy had a history of some sort," Alex went on. "You don't know anything about that?"

Pastor Jeff tilted his head, looking genuinely confused. "I'm afraid I don't. Though, to be honest, I haven't spoken to Troy much about personal relationships during the year and a half he's worked part-time for the church. I'm afraid I don't always get as much time as I'd like to discuss our staff's personal lives."

Relationship. My mind hadn't jumped to a full-fledged relationship between the two, but I wondered if it could be true. I'd thought of Troy as a fair bit older than Candi, due to his stoic nature, but maybe I was wrong. And if that was the case, could Troy have still held anger or resentment toward Candi, so much so that he might want her dead on her wedding day?

I thought again of Lacey and her snide comment, urging us to go after Troy. Could there have been sisterly jealousy at play, too? The prettier, skinnier sister was getting married, while her old flame still felt enough passion to enter into a heated argument with her. All this happened while Lacey was being publicly slapped away.

Lost in thought, I missed any other questions Alex asked as he moved on to questioning Emily and Ms. Mills.

Suddenly, Ms. Mills shouted at one of the boys, taking all of our attention. "Bryce! Where did you get that? Bring that here. That's not one of ours!"

We all looked to the little blond boy who held a different-looking kind of plastic gun. This one was purple, one solid color, with none of the fluorescent orange or green trim of the others.

"Come get it!" Bryce said to Ms. Mills and then took off behind a rolling chalkboard.

"Bryce!" Pastor Jeff said. "When Ms. Mills tells you to do something, you do it. Now bring that gun here, right this second!"

But I suspected the boys were feeling the exhaustion of the day, too, because Bryce didn't listen. He and his brother snickered from behind the same chalkboard. A second later, Bryce peered around the edge of the chalkboard, held up the purple gun, aimed it straight at his dad, and fired.

But when the fluorescent yellow Nerf bullet launched from the gun, it simply fell at Bryce's feet. It didn't occur to us until a second later, when Pastor Jeff gasped, that something else had launched full-speed out of the toy gun. And only a moment after that, a bright red splotch of blood seeped around a tiny needle, stuck into Pastor Jeff's lavender shirt.

We all took in a collective gasp.

Chapter Seven

ALEX AND I ARRIVED AT the hospital right behind the ambulance. After his son shot him with the needle, Pastor Jeff had quickly yanked it out of his chest and immediately started gasping for air. This time, I hadn't wasted a second calling 911, and because the church was located so close to the hospital, both on the east side of Honeysuckle Grove, Pastor Jeff was still coherent when it arrived.

Tears streaked Emily's face when we found her in the emergency room waiting area.

"Ms. Mills is staying at the church to watch the boys," I told her the moment we found her. Alex had spent an extra minute bagging the toy gun and the needle before we left.

Emily nodded and said between sobs, "They wouldn't let me go in with him, but he couldn't even talk!"

Alex headed toward a set of double doors that read AUTHORIZED PERSONNEL ONLY. "Let me see what I can find out."

Apparently, it paid to have a cop around.

I stood hugging Emily in the ER waiting room for the next several long minutes, assuring her that everything would be okay and that we'd caught it in time.

"But I don't understand." She sniffled. "Why would someone load needles into a toy gun?" Emily

Hawthorne was a small, frail lady in her late thirties. She, like her husband, didn't seem to have an untrusting bone in her body. She shook her head in disbelief over the situation as she continued to cry against my shoulder.

What felt like hours later, Alex reappeared through the emergency room doors. He strode straight for us, his gaze squarely on Emily, and my breath caught in my throat.

He took both her hands in his. "He's going to be okay." His words were gentle, but firm.

I let out a gust of air. I wondered how many times in Alex's line of work he'd had to break the news to families that their loved ones would *not* be okay.

"They have him breathing on a ventilator right now, but the doctor seemed to have some idea of what may have inhibited his breathing and he's trying something now to combat it."

"Was it poison?" The moment the question left my mouth, I realized I shouldn't be asking this in front of Pastor Jeff's wife.

But Alex kept his warm eyes right on Emily and simply said, "We should know more soon."

Still swatting myself for my misstep, I offered, "Hey, why don't I go and get us some coffee?"

They were both quick to take me up on it.

I wove my way through hallways to get to the café in the main hospital lobby, which hopefully promised a better cup than the ER vending machines. The lineup was long, but I didn't care. It gave me time to mentally slap myself again for putting extra worry on Emily's mind.

A tray filled with three coffees in hand, along with a baggie of creamers and sugar, I made my way back through the maze of sterile white hallways toward the ER. As I rounded my second corner, though, I saw a flash of a navy suit with sandy Ken-like coiffed hair. Steve Reinhart was talking with a well-dressed couple, and my knee-jerk reaction was to back up and stay hidden.

Detective Reinhart's baritone voice asked, "And you say she had only known the groom for three months?"

I leaned in closer to the corner, hoping I could catch the conversation. Although I'd only gotten a quick glance, from the looks of things, he was still interviewing Mr. and Mrs. Banks.

"I already explained this to the other officer," Mrs. Banks said. "She loved David Albright with all her heart." She didn't sound as emotional as she had been at the park. Perhaps she was all cried out.

"I thought it was early to get married," Mr. Banks elaborated. "But they were both so eager. David actually proposed after they'd only been dating a couple of weeks. We convinced

Candi to at least wait until the end of the summer, so she'd have the wedding she always dreamed of." Mr. Banks choked on the last few words, which made them hard to decipher.

"All right, well, thank you for telling me more about them, and we will certainly speak with the Albrights as well." Detective Reinhart rustled a paper. "And you say I can catch up with your daughter, Lacey, at your house?"

"Can't you leave Lacey for today?" Mrs. Banks asked. "She was here when they told us Candi died, and she'll be an awful mess about losing her sister."

An awful mess? That certainly wasn't what I remembered of Lacey Banks when she'd answered her door in the black mini dress with her hair perfectly straightened. And if what Mrs. Banks was saying was true, Lacey had heard about her sister's death by that time.

"One more question before I go," Detective Reinhart said.

I wondered if this would be about Troy Offenbach and leaned even closer to try and hear every word.

"Is there anyone you know of who would have wanted to bring harm to your daughter?"

A pause—a long one—and then Mr. Banks said, "What are you implying, officer?"

Detective Reinhart cleared his throat. "Nothing for now," he said in the cool, collected voice of someone who had been interviewing prospective witnesses for years. "At this point, we're looking at all angles to get a full picture of this investigation. They're all standard questions after a death that has occurred in a public space."

His words sounded smooth and believable. I wondered how soon he would have to inform Candi's parents that someone had killed her purposely today.

After a longer silence, finally Detective Reinhart nudged. "Did Candi have any enemies, anyone who she didn't get along with perhaps?"

This time Mrs. Banks answered quickly, her voice indignant. "My Candi had a strong personality, and her wedding day had been especially stressful due to the double-booking. She wasn't her best self, so if you're implying she hadn't been kind to someone—"

"I can assure you, Mrs. Banks, I am not implying anything, certainly not about your daughter's character. I'm speaking here of others' characters. Now, you already told me about Troy Offenbach and his argument with her. But was there anyone else?"

I was annoyed at myself for taking so long in the coffee lineup. If I'd been back here sooner, I might have heard the conversation about Troy Offenbach. There were a few seconds of murmuring I couldn't make out, and then Mr. Banks came back with, "Well, those Albrights never cared for Candi, if you ask me. With their natural food choices and making every piece of clothing from hemp or some such thing, I always got the impression they thought of her as superficial because she liked the odd hamburger and enjoyed fashion." He harrumphed to punctuate the statement.

A note page rustled, and then Detective Reinhart confirmed, "That's Brock and Katrina Albright you're talking about? The groom's parents?"

"That's right," Mrs. Banks said. "If you ask us, David was defying his parents by marrying Candi. Might have even been why the boy had been pushing for such a quick wedding."

Or perhaps to get a piece of the Banks' fortune.

"Right. Okay," Detective Reinhart went on. "I'll certainly be interviewing them as well, but what about a Mr. Hector Banks? I heard there was some contention between him and Candi at the park?"

"Hector?" Mr. Banks laughed like the suggestion was ludicrous, but it sounded strained. "Candi's never had an issue with my younger brother. The Banks all get along just fine." He said the words as though there hadn't been at least twenty witnesses who could attest to the opposite.

"All the same," Detective Reinhart went on, undeterred. "Do you know how I can get a hold of Hector? He left the park before my team could speak with him. We're just tying up some loose ends."

"Detective, we'd really like to get back to our Candi before they take her away." Mrs. Banks sniffled, and for the first time, her voice sounded broken.

Detective Reinhart kept his calm. "Absolutely, Mrs. Banks. Just tell me where I can find Hector, and I'll be on my way. If he's your younger brother, you must have an address for him?"

A pause, and then Mr. Banks spoke. "Oh. Yeah. Sure." Mr. Banks rattled off an address.

I quickly placed my tray of coffees on the floor so I could pull out my phone and type in the address.

As I picked up the coffees again, Detective Reinhart thanked the Banks and said goodbye. He was so fast about it, he almost barreled right into me as he rounded the corner away from them.

Chapter Eight

"OH. UM. HEY! DETECTIVE Reinhart!" I said, like the smooth-talker I was. His easy smile and warm steadying hand on my arm made me momentarily lose my voice, but I did my best to coax a swallow and then finally some words. "I'm so glad to see you! Alex is here, and he has to speak with you immediately. Come on, this way!"

I led him in the other direction, and once I could see that the Banks were gone, and as soon as I'd calmed my racing heart, I told him more. "Pastor Jeff was just accidentally shot with one of those same tiny needles at the church. It was from a toy gun found within the children's ministry supplies." I held myself back from calling it the "murder weapon" even though it took serious effort to do so. "They have him on a ventilator while they're trying to counteract whatever went into his bloodstream."

"They're not using epinephrine, are they?" Detective Reinhart's sandy eyebrows pulled together when he turned to me.

"I don't think so. I only heard about the ventilator."

I studied him from the side. My first glance was at his ring finger, which was bare. Then I looked up to his face and wondered how long he had worked as a detective—whether Captain Corbett had promoted him, or if he'd found his way into the ranks before the crotchety police captain took over a half dozen years ago. He didn't look much older than Alex. Maybe thirty.

He caught me looking, and I quickly looked away and picked up my pace.

Detective Reinhart was clearly still business-minded. "I hope not because the doctor who treated Candi suggested the EpiPen may have delivered the poison into her lungs faster. We won't know for sure, of course, until we hear from the medical examiner."

I kept pace beside Detective Reinhart in silence as the seriousness of this hit me. Not only had Detective Reinhart confirmed that Pastor Jeff could have died—still *could* die—he had also just confirmed that it was, indeed, poison that killed Candi Banks, and not some freak accident with some sort of allergen.

Not only that, but if it was poison, it meant beyond any doubt that Candi's death had been intentional. I was quite certain little Bryce Hawthorne hadn't been the mastermind behind the murder of Candi Banks, and he certainly hadn't meant to hurt his dad.

So then who might have attended Candi's wedding or the church picnic to kill her?

My mind kept returning to three people: Troy Offenbach, who had past contention with Candi, had double-booked the park, and most certainly had access to the children's ministry supplies and toy guns. Then there was Lacey Banks, whose emotions over her sister seemed erratic and jealous at best, and was most certainly the closest person to Candi's shoulder right before the poisoning occurred. And I couldn't forget Uncle Hector, who had been drunk and sneaking into the church supplies only moments before Candi had collapsed. The police were clearly interested in him for a reason. Perhaps his whiskey bottle hadn't been the only item he'd been stashing. What if he had been disposing of a purple toy gun?

Detective Reinhart spoke to Alex a mile a minute as soon as he came into view. "Tell me they didn't give the pastor any epinephrine. It may make his condition much worse."

Alex shook his head. "Dr. Khumalo already had a suspicion about possible interactions, and in fact, the pastor is now breathing on his own. They let his wife, Emily, go in."

I looked around, and sure enough, Emily was no longer near any of the waiting room chairs.

"The administering doctor studied in South Africa," Alex went on. "He said the hyperpigmentation that developed on Jeff Hawthorne's chest and back, along with the anaphylactic symptoms, suggested a plant poisoning he had dealt with before."

"Right," Detective Reinhart said. "That's the same doctor who treated

Candi and indicated her condition had worsened with the epinephrine."

"Dr. Khumalo knew of a nonthreatening antidote from his days in South Africa," Alex said. "It had been too late for Candi, as her lungs had caused brain hypoxia, but not for Jeff Hawthorne."

I recognized the term brain hypoxia from when I'd helped Cooper with book research, but I couldn't for the life of me remember what it meant. I'd have to look that up in Cooper's medical encyclopedia when I got home.

"They plan to keep him overnight to ensure the plant compound clears his system," Alex said.

What I understood most about Alex and Detective Reinhart's spiel was that Pastor Jeff was likely going to be okay.

Detective Reinhart seemed to have forgotten about my presence and went on to relay his own progress. "They're doing an autopsy on Candi

Banks. I'll request they also send a blood sample from Jeff Hawthorne to the lab. I suspect we'll find traces of the same toxin in both of their blood. I don't understand why administering an EpiPen exasperated the problem, but I'm sure we'll find it in their report." After pondering this for a few seconds, he changed topics. "I also interviewed her parents. They confirmed Candi had dated Troy Offenbach for a short time in the spring. She broke up with him when she met David Albright, the groom from this afternoon."

So Candi and Troy had been dating. I reset my brain to try and picture them together. Troy had worked at the church for a year and a half, and Candi, with her brash nature—I just couldn't picture her at church, certainly not at Honeysuckle Grove Community Church.

Detective Reinhart went on about David Albright. "Apparently, the two were madly in love. It was a whirlwind romance, and David proposed within two weeks, but the Bankses encouraged them to wait to marry until at least the end of summer. I'm headed to interview him next. I also have an address for Hector Banks. I planned to head there afterward. Care to join me?"

I wasn't sure where Detective Reinhart's regular partner was, but this sort of investigative work could be a big deal for Alex. As he glanced over at me, I wanted to help in any way I could. "I'll talk to you later," I said to Alex, taking a step away.

Silence followed where Detective Reinhart and Alex looked at each other. It seemed to have just occurred to them that I had been listening to all of their updates.

I quickly took another step back from them, as if I could somehow erase my presence and all the missteps I'd made today. Alex furrowed his brow, but thankfully, neither of them pressed me on why I thought eavesdropping on a police investigation was okay.

Detective Reinhart cleared his throat. "Thank you for all of your help today, Mrs. Beck."

As they turned and left, I couldn't tell whether or not his comment had been sarcastic or simply a dismissal.

Chapter Nine

I FELT LONELY ALL THE way home, but just inside my front door, I at least gained some feline camaraderie.

Hunch hadn't waited at the door for me since I'd been on the case for the Montrose murder, but somehow, he intuitively knew I had involved myself in an investigation again, and he had dragged his cast all the way from the living room to the front door to reward me with his presence for it.

I had a couple of trips yet to make from the Jeep, hauling in the coolers of leftover food from the picnic, but Hunch waited patiently, sniffing each one as though he'd understand all of the days' proceedings from scent alone.

I, in turn, rewarded his patience with one heck of a story. I started at the beginning and told him everything. By the time I'd described all that happened at the park in detail, as well as the accidental poisoning of Pastor Jeff, Hunch was rubbing his head up against my calf. If I wanted a little affection, apparently all I had to do was involve myself in the latest Honeysuckle Grove murder investigation.

After the day I'd had, plus hauling in the leftover potluck food and squeezing every bit of it into the fridge, I slumped into the nearest kitchen chair, exhausted, to tell him the rest.

Hunch mewled, looking up at me as if he wanted onto my lap. This was new. I was tempted to peek outside and see if the sky was lit up with aliens or flying pigs.

Carefully, I lifted him and then continued to stroke the soft fur on his head. He met my eyes and raised his eye whiskers.

Oh. Right. My cat didn't want to cuddle. He wanted to discuss the case.

"All I can tell you is that it was definitely a poisoned needle that killed Candi Banks, and another that injured Pastor Jeff. More like a dart, I suppose, as it was rigged to shoot out of a toy gun. Alex is on the case this time, practically officially, so don't worry. He'll figure it out."

I knew before the words were out of my mouth that this answer wouldn't be good enough for Hunch. He growled and dug his front claws into my thigh.

"Ow! Stop! Okay!" As the pain hit me and I was desperate for it to stop, I realized I could at least speculate about a few more details, so Hunch wouldn't feel like I was simply backing away from investigating. Even if I was doing my best to do just that. "As far as I can tell, there are three main suspects: Troy Offenbach, the church treasurer. He was a past boyfriend of Candi's, and apparently, they argued a lot. She dumped him for her groom, David Albright, which must have hurt Troy's ego, if nothing else. He was the one who booked the park, likely knowing Candi was planning a wedding there because it seems like way too much of a coincidence if he didn't. Plus, he had access to all of the church supplies, including the toy guns. That indicates motive and means as far as I'm concerned. He left the picnic before the police could speak to him. Before the incident, Troy had been involved in every aspect of organizing the picnic. I would have expected him to be the last one there, so that spells out avoidance to me."

I reached for one of the madeleines Amber had baked two days ago from the sealable container on my table. "Then there's Candi's sister, Lacey Banks. I'd peg her to have an angry jealous streak—a girl who'd go to almost any length to prove she's as good as her sister and seemed to show absolutely no remorse after she died." I waved a hand. "Anyway, I might have pegged her as our prime suspect because she'd been tinkering with Candi's hair from the back right before she collapsed, and Lacey could have easily inserted a poisoned needle into her shoulder. But that was before we discovered the murder weapon—the toy gun that fired poisoned needle-like darts that I suspect had been aimed at both Candi and Pastor Jeff." I sighed. "Forensics are dusting it for fingerprints, but my guess is that between Pastor Jeff's twin boys, plus Ms. Mills, who grabbed the gun from the kids, there'll be too many prints to decipher anything worthwhile."

Hunch was letting me pet him again and even purred his encouragement, so I went on.

"Then there's Hector Banks, uncle of the bride. Candi clearly hadn't liked him and had just disrespected him in front of a crowd before she collapsed. Plus, he had been digging around in the church's supplies." That was more than likely to stash his whiskey, but I ignored that fact for the moment. "The police are interested in him for some reason." I nibbled my lip at something else that was bothering me. "Then again, I wonder if he would have been too inebriated to have gotten a straight shot into Candi, one she couldn't have simply pulled out on her own." I took a slow breath and let it out as I thought this over. "The police are heading off to question him, clearly thinking he's the prime suspect. My instincts tell me he may have had motive and even opportunity, but not the means because he wasn't sober enough to make an exact shot."

These were the terms Cooper had always used with Hunch, and his ears perked up at them right away.

"So that brings us back to Troy Offenbach, ex-lover and my guess at the prime suspect. Motive and means for sure. Could he have had opportunity in between his arguing with Candi?" I mused aloud. It wasn't as though I had been watching him the whole time. I'd had my attention divided between Ms. Mills and the children, as well as Hector Banks sneaking into the church supplies.

In that moment, Cooper's cat, the one who had never liked me, actually nuzzled the side of his face up against mine. It was the most love and affection I'd received in the last eight and a half months, and I couldn't seem to fight the tears it brought to my eyes.

My phone buzzed from the kitchen table in front of me, thankfully breaking me from the emotion of the moment before Hunch could catch on and roll his little cat eyes at me. He'd never had much patience for sentimentality.

I flipped my phone over to see a new text from Amber.

‹Cooking tonight?›

It must've meant her mom was feeling better, or at the very least, her focus was no longer on her daughter. I sighed. I'd love to see Amber, but to be honest, I didn't know if I had the energy to drive across town and pick her up. Of course, I knew better than to let Hunch in on my lame excuse and actually angled my phone away from him in the unlikely event that he could read as well as he seemed to understand spoken English.

But before I could type, as if Amber could read my mind, another text popped up.

‹Seth's going out. He can drop me off.›

Seth was Amber's older brother. When I'd first met her, she'd been calling him Danny Jr. after their dad, but after all they'd learned about what their dad had been involved with prior to his death, Amber clearly no longer blamed her brother for going by his middle name of Seth.

‹Sure› I typed back, barely taking the time to think about it.

I was too tired to cook, too tired to teach cooking, and there was far too much food in my cluttered fridge already.

However, I'd sooner eat fried worms with gravy than turn down a friend who wanted to come over and keep me company.

Chapter Ten

AMBER ARRIVED HALF AN hour later, and it was all I could do not to hug the fifteen-year-old I'd only met three weeks ago. Not only that, but Hunch's allegiance turned on a dime the moment Amber crossed my threshold into my house. He mewled beside her legs in the kitchen until she picked him up and gave him some love. He lapped it up, like he hadn't felt human touch in a year.

Amber looked fresh out of the shower, with less-curly-than-normal damp hair, and a red tank top that read IT'S NOT ME, IT'S YOU.

"How's your mom?" I asked.

Amber shrugged. "Medicated."

I nodded. This was Helen Montrose's approach to grief, which left her two teenage kids mostly fending for themselves. "If you ever need to talk about anything, Amber, you know you don't always have to be strong around me, right?"

Amber shrugged one shoulder, which I thought meant she was too uncomfortable by this subject, but then she said, "Sometimes I have panic attacks, like where I can't breathe."

"Just since your dad died?" I asked. She nodded. "I had them for a while after I lost Cooper. I kept a paper bag with me for months. Have you tried breathing into one? It helps a bit. Or breathing through a straw."

"I'll try that." She looked down at Hunch and continued stroking him. I hated to admit it, but that cranky cat was certainly good for something, or at least someone.

"And you know you can always call me," I added. "Even in the middle of the night."

"So I can talk to your voicemail?" She smirked. She knew I hadn't had a home phone since shortly after Cooper died, but she didn't know how neurotic I still was with my cell phone. I figured it was only fair if I reciprocated in putting myself out there.

"Ever since Cooper died, I can't seem to turn off my phone. I always keep it on, even at night. Even though Cooper died in the middle of the day, I don't know, each night when I get into bed, I put down my phone and think, 'What if something happened to my dad in the night? Or my sister?' Even if you just feel lonely, call me. Okay?"

Amber shrugged, which I was pretty sure meant she was agreeing. But she was done with this soul-bearing conversation. "So that bride is really dead, huh?" she asked, leaning against my kitchen counter. It only occurred to me now how out of the loop Amber was on this. Usually, her quick fifteen-year-old brain kept at least one step ahead of me at every turn. It made me feel strangely uneasy to know I held all the info from today on my own.

"Yeah, not only that, but Pastor Jeff was shot with the same type of needle." Her eyes widened with horror, so I quickly amended, "He's going to be fine. The needle did contain a poison, or what the doctors are calling a 'plant toxin,' but they counteracted it in plenty of time."

"Wait, what?" Amber shook her head as though she had flying insects in her hair. "Somebody shot Pastor Jeff at the park after I left?"

Whoops. I obviously had to backtrack. I waved my hands and said, "No, no, later at the church with the kids and the toys and..."

Amber's horror-stricken face told me I really needed to start at the beginning.

"Okay, listen. Remember when you first arrived at the park and there was an upset between the bride and Troy from the church about a double-booking?"

Amber nodded hesitantly, but at least she was with me now. I led her to two kitchen chairs at the table, opened the cookie container, and went through every detail from the park to the church to the hospital, bit by bit.

Hunch looked just as engaged as he had the last time I'd recounted this story. Except this time, he gave all of his affection to Amber for it.

When I got to the end, about the three suspects I had narrowed it down to, and that the police seemed more interested in Uncle Hector than they did with Troy Offenbach, even though in my opinion, Troy or Lacey were clearly the prime suspects, Amber slumped back into her chair and simply said, "Wow."

"I know, right?" There was only one madeleine left in the cookie container, but all this talk made me want to nibble. I hesitated, knowing I should really leave it for my guest—the person who had baked them, after all. But if I didn't find something to do with my hands soon, I'd be up at the counter cooking off my anxiousness instead. Heaven knew I didn't need any more food. I reached for the cookie.

"What about the Albrights?" Amber asked.

"What's that?" I asked around a mouthful of cookie.

"Troy Offenbach seems too obvious to me. You said the Albrights never liked Candi. I can't remember who said that."

"Mr. and Mrs. Banks," I put in, "but they're both such different families with different affluence. It makes sense if their families aren't exactly besties."

Amber shrugged. "Could be some kind of a family spat, though. I'd look into them before I'd focus on some church treasurer who wasn't hiding his anger and frustration at Candi from anyone that day."

Hmm. What she said made sense. It would be one thing if Troy had gotten so heated and angry that he'd grabbed a rock in the heat of the moment and struck Candi over the head with it or something. But the toy gun, reworked so it could launch toxic needles...that was premeditated. And if Troy had premeditated the murder, why would he have been publicly arguing with Candi only moments before her death? Why would Uncle Hector or Lacey have done that, for that matter? Unless one of them hoped to get caught.

Huh. In all of ten seconds, Amber Montrose had all but exonerated all three of my suspects. Maybe I wasn't so good at this investigative work after all.

"So if it was someone like the Albrights..." Or someone else, entirely, I thought but didn't say. My mind raced through hundreds of people who had flown under my radar at the park Sunday afternoon and who hadn't been cleared by the police. "I suppose I should call Alex and suggest the police look into them."

Hunch growled, which was nothing new, but it seemed by Amber's pursed lips, she didn't think I should hand this suggestion over to the police just yet either.

"You said this Reinhart guy's in charge, right?" Amber asked.

I stupidly felt my cheeks flush at his name, remembering how stupid I'd felt after getting caught eavesdropping on his and Alex's conversation. Amber fiddled with the lid on the cookie container, and I was tempted to apologize for greedily scarfing down the last one. But this conversation was much more important, so I only nodded.

"I don't know if I'm right about the Albrights," Amber said, "and we don't want Alex making bad suggestions if he's trying to win some favor with the local detective squad."

That made a lot of sense. I was glad I had this smart kid in my corner to think of these things. "So what do we do?" I asked.

Amber stood from her chair and paced back and forth in my open kitchen a few times, pondering this. She stopped at the fridge, opened the door wide, and stood in front of it, twisting her lips to the side.

Again, I felt awful for eating the last cookie. I moved behind her to find something I could heat up quickly. Most of the sweets and desserts had been picked up by their church-going owners.

But then Amber asked, "You said the Bankses didn't want any of the food from the picnic?"

I thought back to how offended Lacey Banks had been at even the suggestion. "Nope."

"Well..." Amber looked over her shoulder at me, and the refrigerator light illuminated her face in a way that made her look mischievous. She pulled out a casserole dish and peeked inside. "Maybe the Albrights do."

Chapter Eleven

I DIDN'T KNOW IF AMBER was correct in her suggestions, but with an entire park full of people to investigate, and only two detectives and Alex—who couldn't yet make his own decisions—on the case, I figured anyone we could look into that might slip by the police's immediate notice might help.

Besides, the Bankses and the Albrights couldn't be more different. It wasn't simply a matter of money, either. The Bankses had a superficial consciousness about them, and thinking back to David Albright's mother in her sack-dress and messy braids, she seemed to be the opposite of Mrs. Banks in every way.

After a long discussion about this, and spending some time investigating both families online, Amber spent the night at my place. Her mom had OK'ed it, but one of these days, I suspected Mrs. Montrose would emerge from her fog of grief and want to actually get to know the adult woman who had all but adopted her daughter.

"There's only one Albright in the local directory," Amber said first thing the next morning from the kitchen table, scrolling on her phone.

I finished wiping the counter and came to look over her shoulder. Recognition struck, and I nodded. "That's them, Brock and Katrina Albright. I remember Detective

Reinhart mentioning their first names to Alex."

"You're sure?" Amber asked. I nodded.

There had been almost a weekly account of the Banks family in the local paper—everything from the Banks Jewelers locations they owned throughout the state, to Candi's cheerleading accolades from high school two years ago. Last week's online news had spoken of the Banks wedding, but Amber scanned the entire article and didn't see a single instance of the name "Albright."

That got us searching specifically for the Albrights, but they were clearly not newsworthy people. The only instance I could find while googling "Brock Albright" with "West Virginia" was a building permit from twelve years ago for a free-standing structure.

To be honest, it surprised me that the quiet, keep-to-themselves people were listed in the local phone book, but I was glad to have their address.

Amber stood to check on our casserole in the oven. Even though we had more food in the fridge than two people could eat in a week, we had both decided last night to get up early and make a fresh casserole for the Albrights. This one was vegan and filled with the remainder of fresh vegetables from my fridge. From what Mr. Banks had indicated, the Albrights seemed like a family that lived and ate naturally. When Amber peeked into the oven and saw the vegan cheese sauce bubbling, she turned on the frying pan, ready to crisp up some onions for the top. "Why don't you get ready while I finish this up?"

Sometimes I'd swear Amber was the adult—not to mention the chef—in the house, and I was the teenager. But in an effort to bring the Albrights a wonderfully fresh and warm casserole that might get them talking to us, I followed her instructions and ran up the stairs.

Half an hour later, Amber and I drove to the outskirts of Honeysuckle Grove, following my GPS to a small house that was nestled between two farms. The Albrights' tiny farmhouse sat on a small plot of land, surrounded by a weathered picket fence. Shrubbery was snug up to the right-hand side of the house, while the left side had a large walnut tree, along with about a six-foot-wide "path" of thigh-high grass leading up to a tall fence.

"I wonder if they work on one of the neighboring farms or have some sort of crop on their own out back," I said, surveying the area.

Amber passed me the warm casserole. "Why don't you take it in on your own and ask them? I'll snoop around outside a bit while you have them distracted. See if there's anything out of place."

I nodded, but I was starting to have my doubts about this plan and about the Albrights as serious suspects. This house suited them in every way—from the walnut tree in their front yard to the dreamcatcher hanging over the front porch. They seemed like such simple people who lived a simple life. Sure, they were different from the Bankses, but that didn't make the two families sworn enemies.

Maybe the most we should expect was finding out some intel about who David and Candi spent time with. I hoped we'd even get to speak to David today. He was certainly young enough that he could still live with his parents, and the police had already done their questioning of the groom, so I didn't feel as guilty about looking into him myself.

Still, I had this fresh and warm casserole, constructed specifically for them. The least I could do was deliver it.

Amber and I got out on either side of the Jeep. Amber stayed in a crouch as she moved around the Albright's old beater truck and toward the left side of the house. I took the casserole up the three cement steps to the front door.

The house must have been at least forty years old. The paint looked as though it used to be white, but it was chipped so extensively, it was hard to tell. Even the small patch of lawn in the front yard needed a cut, or more likely a sickle. I wondered what the Albrights spent their time on if they weren't able to keep up on their house and yard.

It seemed the doorbell was broken, so after a long minute of waiting, I knocked. It was Mr. Albright—Brock—who answered. He wore baggy jeans and a plaid short-sleeve shirt. His clothing was worn and looked at least a couple of decades old. His pale forearms and face gave me doubts that he would spend enough time in the sun to work as a farmer.

In his arms, he held a box that was a little bigger than a shoebox. The flaps were folded down over one another, so I couldn't see inside, even when he held it outstretched toward me.

"Mr. Albright?" I asked.

He clued in that the reason I wasn't accepting his outstretched box was because I held a casserole dish in my hands. He looked between the dish and my face several times before pulling the box back toward himself.

Now it was my turn to outstretch the casserole. "Hi!" I said in much too perky and high-pitched of a voice for the reason of my visit. I cleared my throat and dropped my tone. "Um, I'm from Honeysuckle Grove Community Church?" Brock Albright simply furrowed his brow, either not recognizing the name or not understanding why I was bothering him, so I went on. "Our church just felt awful about what happened at your son's wedding yesterday, and we wanted to deliver a casserole." I held the warm dish out another inch toward him.

He pulled the box away and stuffed it under an arm and turned away from me without another word. As he walked away, he called out, "Katrina? The church sent us a casserole."

The lady in braids—Katrina Albright—appeared in the doorway only a moment later. Her blonde braids had loosened and frayed, and I wondered if she hadn't re-braided them since before the wedding yesterday. If not for the yellow collar on her dress, I'd think it was the same beige sack-dress she'd worn to the wedding as well.

"I'm Mallory Beck, from the church that was at the park yesterday," I said, hoping this might make more sense. "We just wanted to do anything we could to make this time easier for everyone involved." I held out the casserole toward her.

Thankfully, Mrs. Albright was quick to don a smile and reach for it. "Oh, isn't that nice." She looked back at the hallway where her husband had disappeared. "That's so nice of them, isn't it, Brock?" she called, but there was no answer. Mrs. Albright accepted the warm casserole from my hands, tilted her head, and said, "Would you like to come in, dear?"

She had to be about forty. Not really old enough that I'd expect her to call me "dear," but I did want to come in.

"Oh, maybe just for a minute," I said.

Katrina Albright lingered, leading me slowly through their

entryway to a small living room. There were a dozen photos of a young David along a hearth, each framed in a hand-chiseled frame. Handmade crocheted blankets covered the back of every couch and chair, and the whole place had a homemade feel. Behind the couch, one wall held a large framed painting that looked like it could have been created by a grade-schooler. It was of a family of three—a man and boy with dark hair, and a woman in golden braids. The details were wonky, but not in an abstract sort of way. More like the perspective and depth was attempted by someone not very proficient with a paintbrush.

Katrina sat on the edge of an armchair so I dropped into the couch.

"Is David your only child?" I asked. The more I looked around, the more I saw knickknacks on every surface that looked handmade, and possibly by a child—from the rudimentary metalwork helicopter on the windowsill to the simple wooden shelf on the wall.

"Yes," Katrina said with a beaming smile. "We always wanted more children, but David is what God gave us."

I had never seen the Albrights at Honeysuckle Grove Community Church, which was by far the largest church in town. I wondered if they attended the tiny Seventh Day Adventist Church in town or the Catholic one.

I looked around the room. "Had David already moved in with Candi?" I said her name somberly, as felt natural of the newly deceased.

Katrina's smile didn't decrease any. "Oh, no. Before they were married?" she asked as a rhetorical question. I wasn't sure if I was imagining the edge to her voice. In general, she seemed like such a simple clear-cut lady who wasn't hiding a thing. But maybe there was one thing...

"So he still lives here?" I looked around again, as though David might materialize from somewhere within the small house. He couldn't be much over twenty. It wouldn't be unusual for him to still be living with his parents. Brock hadn't reappeared either, and I wondered where he was hiding, as the house didn't look very large from the outside. I hoped wherever it was, he didn't have a vantage point of Amber sneaking around his backyard.

"Well, not really, not at the moment," Katrina said. She lifted a plate of cookies from the hand-carved coffee table to offer me one. I was a big fan of cookies of any kind and was always curious about other people's recipes. I helped myself. But after only one bite, I wanted to put it back. The rough texture of it felt and tasted like sawdust.

"Mmm," I said, more in an effort to coax some saliva than to compliment her. "What's in your cookies?"

Katrina beamed and nodded. "Hemp and walnut. All grown right here on our land."

A knock sounded at the front door, and before either Katrina or I could even look in that direction, Brock whisked down the hallway with the same cardboard box and opened it. I could see the hallway, but couldn't quite see him or whoever was on the other side.

A moment later, though, the door closed, and I watched through their front window as Brock walked a young woman about my age who looked a little scruffy in ripped jeans and a black T-shirt back toward the driveway, where a red hatchback was parked. The woman nodded at whatever Brock was telling her as they walked.

I took another bite of my cookie, momentarily forgetting the dryness, and swallowed hard to get it down my throat. At the red car, Brock passed the box to the woman, and she passed him an envelope. If we were somewhere other than nature-ville, I'd swear I was witnessing a drug deal.

Then again, maybe these people ran a grow-op somewhere on their property. I thought of Amber, sneaking around, and willed Brock Albright to keep his focus on his current conversation.

"Another cookie?" Katrina asked, interrupting my thoughts.

That was the last thing I wanted, and so my eyes darted around the room, looking for some way to quickly change the subject. In the corner of the room, I noticed one item that looked out of place from all the homemade knickknacks. It was a bright green lava lamp, definitely store-bought.

"Is that yours?" I asked, pointing. As usual, the words were out of my mouth before I thought of how they might sound. "I mean, it's really pretty." Not much better, considering the cord was dangling nearby, unplugged, not looking all that pretty in its current state.

Katrina sighed. "My mother sends David gifts from England on his birthday each year. I tried to make her understand we preferred homemade items, but that was the closest she seemed to be able to get to the idea." She sighed again.

"So you were mentioning that David doesn't live with you?" I said, fishing. If he'd moved out, why was his lava lamp still here? "What is he, about twenty?"

Katrina's forehead buckled, and she nodded. She was on her third cookie, and I wondered how she swallowed one after another without any water in sight. "He turned eighteen in the spring. He's been moving his things into the new house he planned to share with Candi for weeks. He stayed there last night." She looked down at the floor, and her forehead creased even further.

"It must be awful for him," I said. Eighteen? He was just a kid.

Brock appeared in the entry to the living room and cleared his throat. I hadn't even noticed him return to the house. "We need to water the gardens, sweetheart." His words sounded as though they came through gritted teeth.

Mrs. Albright popped up out of her seat in an instant. "Oh, yes, of course."

It seemed inviting me inside the house had only been a nicety, not one she thought I'd actually accept. I hadn't seen much in the way of kept gardens in the front yard. Amber would know by now if they had one in the back, and if there was anything interesting in their yard.

"Oh. Well. I should be going anyway," I said. An idea came to me, and I said it aloud before I could rethink it. "If David's living at his new place, perhaps I could get the address and deliver a meal to him as well?"

"You told her David wasn't living here?" Brock narrowed his eyes at his wife.

Katrina glanced at her husband, but she responded to me rather than to him. "Oh, that's so nice of you." She wore another smile, but this one looked less genuine. "Why don't you just drop it off here? David should be back soon."

I nibbled the inside of my cheek. Was I just imagining it, or was she trying to keep me from seeing her son? But I couldn't think of any way of pushing the matter, so I stood and headed for the door.

"Yes, okay. I'll do that. I hope you enjoy this one." I didn't know what else to say, and when I got to the door, I saw Amber in the front seat of the Jeep where I'd parked along the road. She was on her phone.

"Oh, I'm sure we will, dear," Katrina said.

"Did you take one to the Bankses yet?" Brock's feelings toward the family were quite clear in his gruff tone as he pronounced their name.

I tilted my head, willing to feed this fire at least a little before I left. "Oh, believe me, I tried. They didn't want any part of what they thought was my charity." I sighed as I watched Brock and Katrina's reaction carefully. "I tried to make them understand that I just wanted to make things easier on them, but..." I looked down and shook my head.

Brock's face deepened into a scowl. "Shoulda probably delivered it to Hector Banks. Told him it was a celebratory casserole."

I put a hand to my chest and faked shock, even though his feelings about the Banks uncle didn't really surprise me. "Oh? Did Hector Banks dislike Candi?"

Brock Albright snickered, and his nostrils flared. "That guy only likes two things—his whiskey and his guns."

Brock didn't give me a chance to ask him about this. He disappeared somewhere inside the house again, apparently satisfied that I was leaving.

I pasted on a smile, thanked Katrina for the cookie, and said goodbye.

At least I had an invitation to come back, if need be.

Chapter Twelve

AMBER HUNG UP THE phone as I got into the Jeep.

"Who were you calling?" I asked as I put the Jeep in drive and headed toward town.

"The municipal office," she said. "Maybe you were right about Troy Offenbach being our prime suspect. Maybe I was looking for something more complicated that wasn't there."

"Why? What did you find out?"

She scrolled through something on her phone as she spoke. "Troy was definitely the person who booked the church picnic at the park, but the lady at the municipal office said he specifically asked for only one shelter, even though the church had always rented both shelters for every picnic they'd had in the past."

I was about to interrupt, to say that didn't automatically make him a murderer, but she had more to tell me.

"The other strange part was that he insisted the bill for the shelter and park rental get mailed to him directly, and not to the church."

"Huh." What amazed me more than this new information was how quickly my allegiance or blame for someone could flip-flop back and forth. But this certainly was something to look into. "I should text Alex and see if the police have tracked Troy down at home to question him."

"You're going to have to," Amber said, clicking off her phone and looking at me. "There are no Offenbachs listed in the online directory, and Penny at the church wouldn't give me his number or address."

"He's unlisted?" Something my dad had said every time we moved to a new town when I was growing up was that people who had nothing to hide listed themselves in the local phone book. I'd thought it was a waste of time for us, as we often didn't end up staying long in each town, but he always insisted. Again, though, I had to remind myself that this wasn't actually proof of guilt. "Anything else?" I asked. I was trying to train myself to get all the facts before convincing myself of my wild theories.

"Nah. I snuck around the back of the Albright's farmhouse, but their entire backyard is taken up by a gigantic greenhouse or something— except it's covered in black plastic."

Maybe I wasn't so far off in my grow-op theory. Still, it certainly didn't make the Albrights murderers. "Brock didn't see you when he went down the driveway with that woman?" I asked.

She shook her head. "No, but funny enough, I'd been trying to figure out a way to get over the tall fence to their backyard because it was locked. Right after the woman drove away, Brock headed straight for the back fence. I had to scramble to get behind a tree so he didn't see me."

My eyes widened. I wondered what a man like Brock might have done if he'd found Amber snooping around, especially if he kept an illegal grow-op back there.

But Amber went on like this was all no big deal. "He was only back there for a minute, but it was long enough for me to jam my gum into the lock so it wouldn't click all the way shut when he came back through it. As soon as he went back into the house, I went for a quick look, but the greenhouse was locked, too." She shrugged. "They could be growing marijuana or coca plants for cocaine, for all we know, but that still wouldn't make them murderers." Exactly my hypothesis. "Anything interesting inside their house?"

"It could have definitely been a drug deal with the red car. None of the neighboring farms would be keeping an eye from their distance away. I doubt he would be on the police's radar way out here in farmland. But like you say, that wouldn't make them murderers." I turned onto Amber's street. "Mr. Albright barely said two words to me until I was leaving, when he told me Hector Banks only liked two things: his whiskey and his guns."

"Guns?" Amber raised her eyebrows. "Even though it was a toy gun, what kind of person would take the time to restructure one to shoot poisoned darts?" She didn't leave me time to answer. "We should check and see if Alex interviewed Hector Banks yet."

I nodded. It was what I planned to do as soon as I got home. "Katrina Albright was nice enough. David is an only child and seems like their pride and joy. Apparently, he's been staying at the house he'd planned to move into with Candi, but they wouldn't tell me where that was."

"So they were evasive?" Amber asked.

"I guess. Mostly I think Brock Albright just wanted me out of their house. He said something about needing to water the plants, so that makes sense if they have some kind of extensive greenhouse in the backyard."

"None of it makes sense if you ask me," Amber said as I pulled up to her house. When we'd been sneaking around together, investigating her dad's murder, I'd always dropped her off and picked her up down the street at the corner. Something about pulling right into her driveway still felt wrong, but I took a deep breath and reminded myself I wasn't doing anything underhanded here.

But then Amber said, "I'll hang out here for a bit, let Mom know I'm around, then I'll sneak out again later. In the meantime, why don't you get the story about Hector Banks from Alex? Also, you should get Troy Offenbach's address out of him."

Sometimes I forgot that Amber was only fifteen. Other times, like now, when she talked about sneaking out of her house and talking a police officer into giving up info about a murder suspect, it was glaringly obvious.

"I'll see what I can do," I told her sarcastically, then waved goodbye before driving home.

I texted Alex, asking him to check in when he had a chance, but didn't get an immediate reply, so I spent the rest of the morning contacting folks from the church about the dishes they'd left behind at the church picnic. Most of them suggested I could go ahead and eat the food and they'd get their dishes back the next Sunday. I hated wasting food, and as I transferred each item to my own dish, I wondered again what I would do with it all. Even if Amber moved in for the week, the two of us wouldn't be able to consume it all, and I didn't think much of it would do well in the freezer.

I was just heading back for the fridge to pull out another armful of potluck dishes when the doorbell rang. Hunch, who hadn't given me the time of day since Amber left, perked up his ears and dragged his cast toward the front door. I made it there before him and opened the door to find Alex on the other side.

"Oh! Hi," I said too enthusiastically. My brain ricocheted to all the information I was supposed to pry out of my cop friend—Hector Banks's story, Troy Offenbach's address, what he'd found out from

David Albright—but then I mentally slapped myself for the thoughts. I wasn't in the habit of using people, especially my friends, and besides, Alex's forehead was creased. His eyes looked dark and troubled. "Is everything okay? Come on in," I said instead.

Alex reached down to scratch the fur around Hunch's neck and then followed me to the kitchen. "Whoa!" he said the moment we moved through the doorway. "I wasn't meaning to invite myself for lunch, but..."

"Hey, if you're hungry, you'd be doing me a huge favor to eat some of this up." I had most of the casserole and side dishes out on my counter to figure out what to do with them. I got a microwave-safe plate from the cupboard and passed that, along with a spoon, over to Alex. "Help yourself."

He served himself a heaping plate, and I followed along, filling my own much smaller plate. I wasn't sure if I should ask again, but I couldn't seem to help myself. "So...you didn't answer me. Is everything okay?"

Alex heaved in a big breath and let it out. "I suppose. Just another run-in with Corbett. He found out I'd been assisting with the investigation and gave Reinhart an earful about it." He shook his head at the floor. "The stuff he assigns me is work made for kindergarteners. I shouldn't be surprised. The attribution of work at the station has never been anywhere near even. I should have probably backed out gracefully, or told Corbett I'd wheedled my way into it, something so Reinhart wouldn't take the heat. But I just sat there. Now not only is Corbett trying to keep me away from the detective unit, Reinhart's back to relying on his regular partner, Detective Bernard, who is far too busy to conduct all of the interviews plus deal with forensics."

I slid Alex's full plate into the microwave and set it to heat for a minute. "I don't get it. Why does Corbett have it out for you? You seem like you're trying so hard to get along in the department."

Alex had mentioned it had been his dad, once a cop within the local department, who'd instigated the problem, but he'd never given me any details. I, of anyone, knew how hard it could be to talk about parents and their inadequacies, and I hoped he was learning he could trust me.

He helped himself to his plate from the microwave, and I slid mine in. He dropped into a chair at the table before he spoke again. "My dad, he wasn't the get-along type. He made lots of enemies within the department before he left."

"And Corbett was one of them?" I confirmed, taking my own plate from the microwave and sitting across from him. I already knew this part, but I wanted to keep the conversation going.

Alex shrugged. "For all I know, he's the only one who still has a grudge against him, but Dad was pretty famous for ruffling feathers. Corbett was new in town after our old captain, Ron Salinger, retired. Dad pretty much ran the department himself when Salinger still officially called the shots, so you could say the transition wasn't exactly seamless. Dad and Corbett were both type A personalities. I was fresh out of the academy and trying to work my way up, but it seemed every time Dad had a run-in with Corbett, I found myself on grunt duty or with a mound of extra paperwork. Since Dad transferred out of Honeysuckle Grove, things are better than they were. Just not much room for advancement, you know?"

"Well...did anyone officially tell you that you were off the Candi Banks' murder investigation?"

He shrugged as he finished chewing another big bite. "I guess not, but it's only because I'm waiting to hear back from interview subjects and the medical examiner's office. Reinhart's been running the interviews, Bernard has been balancing his forensics work with his work on another case, and so I was hoping to continue to fill in, but I don't want to be too visible about it or push my luck."

"Well, good," I told Alex. I had yet to take a bite. If Alex was upset, I couldn't think about eating, but I hoped he could see that there might still be a light at the end of the tunnel for him here. "Keep at it quietly then. Does Reinhart know Corbett's problem is really with your dad? And why does Corbett keep hanging your dad's issues over your head if your dad's gone?"

"Everyone knows," Alex said, and then took another big bite. I had to wait for him to chew and then swallow. He clearly had no trouble stomaching food, no matter the amount of stress or emotional upheaval in his life. Finally, he added, "There was a big blowout before Dad left. No one else was there to hear what Corbett actually said, but Dad stormed out, saying he couldn't work with a racist captain and was going to the mayor."

My eyes widened. No wonder Corbett hated the Martinez family, and vice versa.

"Dad couldn't prove anything, and so next thing I knew, he had a job offer down in Charlotte—a good one as chief investigator. I suspect either the mayor or Corbett pulled some strings to get him out of here."

I shook my head and took my first bite, mostly because I didn't know what to say to that. By the time I had swallowed, all I had come up with was, "Too bad you want to stay in Honeysuckle Grove."

"Heh. Yeah, too bad." His response only pointed out how lame my reassurance was.

It seemed like a no-win situation, and so I decided to open up about my own family's no-win situation. "My dad didn't exactly make my life easy, either," I told him. "When I was growing up, my dad got fired so often, I didn't have a chance to get attached to any one town."

Alex tilted his head, like he truly had compassion for me, even in the midst of his much worse turmoil.

"Until now," I said. He stared at me for so long, I looked down and added, "I'm getting pretty attached to Honeysuckle Grove." My cheeks warmed, hoping he wouldn't realize that he was at least half the reason for that. It had been the same in seventh grade.

Alex stood and went to help himself to another plate of food. I was glad he felt comfortable enough to do so. "So if I'm committed to this town, and you're committed to this town," he said, "I guess we just have to find a way to work around any little annoyances."

Little annoyances. I loved how he played down his serious work struggles. "So is that why you came by? To talk about Corbett and Reinhart?"

"Oh. Right. All this food, and I'd momentarily forgotten about the reason for my visit." He smirked over his shoulder at me as he heaped another large spoonful of macaroni and cheese onto his plate. "I wanted to update you on the case."

I scrunched my forehead. "Really?"

"Sure. Well, I mean, I wanted to ask your opinion on something, too."

That didn't clear my confusion up. Again, I had to ask, "Really?" Shouldn't he play it carefully if he wanted to wedge his way into Honeysuckle Grove Police

Department's detective unit? And what could he possibly need from me?

"Steve and I finally found Hector Banks late last night. He has a record, and his fingerprints were a match to both the church's Rubbermaid bin and the whiskey bottle. We haven't been able to match a print from the toy gun yet, though."

"A record?"

Alex shrugged. "Just some breaking and entering, petty theft stuff, but Reinhart was familiar with his name as soon as the wedding planner mentioned it. It took us a while to locate him, which tends to happen when someone is hiding in plain sight."

"Oh, yeah? Was he at the address Candi's parents gave to Detective Reinhart?" I wasn't comfortable calling Detective Reinhart Steve yet, but it seemed Alex calling him by his first name was a good sign, a sign there wasn't too much animosity between them.

"Not only was he not there, he moved out the month before. We spoke to his landlord, and get this, his forwarding address was the same as Candi and her parents." Alex sat across from me with his second heaping plate.

"Weird. And so you went back to their house next?" I recalled visiting the house and hearing voices inside before the door opened to a very evasive Lacey Banks.

"We did. We actually ran surveillance for a couple of hours, just watching who came and went, to get a sense of the family, as it seems they're trying to keep some secrets."

"Did you find out anything?" I asked between bites of delicious eggplant parmesan. I made a mental note to look up who had baked it.

"We saw the Bankses arrive home from the hospital, still looking quite broken up about their daughter. That's when Hector appeared out on their front stoop. He wore slippers and held a near-empty liquor bottle, like he'd been inside their house drinking the whole time. They had an animated argument with him. We couldn't hear any of it, but all three of them looked upset. Of course, that was to be expected. We were about to go and get some clear answers out of all of them when we saw the younger daughter, Lacey Banks, sneak out from a side door of the large house."

I'd stopped eating. Even the best eggplant parmesan in the world couldn't take my rapt attention from this story. "None of the other Bankses saw her? Where'd she go?"

He raised his eyebrows. "That's what we wanted to know. We were down the street, watching their house with binoculars. When Lacey snuck along a side path toward a neighbor's house, we decided to back up and follow her. She ended up getting picked up by a group of young people in a convertible. Steve got the plate number, and he's looking into it. We wouldn't have been able to follow them without being noticed, but the strangest part was that Lacey, as well as all the others in the car, were laughing when they left."

"Laughing?" I raised my eyebrows in disbelief. "The day her sister died? Was she still in the black mini dress?"

"Yeah. It seemed almost like a celebration. So that's weird, right?" Alex looked at me with furrowed eyebrows, like his question was a serious one.

"Yeah, that's weird. *That's* what you wanted to ask me about?" I was beyond confused. Alex wasn't stupid, not by any stretch of the imagination, so why was he asking a stupid question?

He shrugged. "I know you've been hanging around with Amber. She's, what, seventeen?"

I smiled inwardly. Amber would be incredibly pleased to be mistaken for seventeen. "Fifteen," I told him.

"Mm. Okay." He nodded and shrugged. "Lacey Banks is eighteen. I thought you might have some insight into that age group, losing someone close to them, you know, because of Amber."

I took another bite and thought that over. "There's a big difference between fifteen and eighteen, and I suspect a big difference in the girls' personalities as well, so I'm not sure I can be of much help, but I'm quite certain Amber still hasn't been going out with friends and joking around. She spends most evenings over at my house learning how to cook." I hadn't actually thought of that as part of her grieving process for her dad, but it would make sense if it was.

Still, I felt like this comparison would get us nowhere.

"That's all the confirmation I need. I'll definitely look closer at Lacey Banks."

I opened my mouth, then hesitated, wondering if I should nudge him to look into Troy. But maybe Amber was right and nudging him in the wrong direction, before we had any substantial proof, might be bad for Alex's career, especially after everything he told me about his tenuous place in the department. "Did you eventually get to question Hector?"

Alex shook his head. "We went back and banged on the Bankses' door. They insisted Hector wasn't inside and they hadn't seen him. They wouldn't let us in the house, so Steve's requesting a warrant." Alex let out a sigh. "This kind of thing's pointless, though. By the time we get the warrant, Hector Banks will be long gone from their house. All it proves is that the Bankses clearly have something to hide."

Alex had finished his second full plate of food and returned to the counter for a little more of the eggplant parmesan. He had good taste. He leaned back against the counter, waiting for it to get nuked. Maybe I wouldn't have to worry so much about the surplus of food with Alex around.

After all Alex had told me, and so freely, I felt a little guilty about Amber's idea to look into Troy behind his back, even if we did plan to pass on any information once we found it. The least I could do was tell him what we'd done today.

"Amber and I delivered a casserole to the Albright house this morning."

Alex's eyebrows shot up, but he'd just sat down and taken a large bite of his eggplant parm, so he chewed and swallowed before he asked, "Why'd you do that?"

I shrugged. I wasn't sure if he wanted me to admit that we'd been doing our own investigating, or if he'd reprimand me for it. "We figured they must be grieving, too, and they're not nearly as well off as the Banks family."

Alex nodded. "Steve and I haven't gotten over there yet, but we interviewed their son at the hospital. We didn't learn much, as he was a blubbering mess, clearly upset about the death of his bride. Learn anything interesting from his parents?"

I described the farmhouse with the peeling paint, overgrown grass, and a greenhouse in the back. "Apparently, David had been moving his things into the house he'd planned to share with Candi. His parents figured he was grieving, and he'd be back to live with them shortly, but they didn't seem to want to give me the address of where David was staying."

Alex smirked at me. He knew I'd gone there to investigate.

"I said I wanted to bring David a casserole," I explained. "But Katrina

Albright insisted it would be better if I dropped it off with them."

"So David still spends a lot of time at their house, I assume?" Alex asked.

I shrugged. "They didn't seem to be in agreement about that, but I can tell you that their precious son is in every wall hanging and knickknack in that house." I went on to explain how David was Brock and Katrina's only son.

Alex nodded along with my story as he polished off his third plate.

"But the most interesting part of the morning was when Brock Albright started talking about Hector Banks. Said he didn't like Candi and, in fact, only liked two things: his whiskey and his guns."

Alex stopped mid-bite. "His guns?"

I nodded. "I definitely think it's worth tracking down Hector to ask him a few questions."

"Steve and I have talked extensively about whether or not Hector, in his drunken state, had the ability to aim a gun so specifically and be able to conceal the whole event, but you're right. He's worth looking into. Especially if he could have been grossly exaggerating his state of drunkenness."

I thought back. I had been a few mere feet away from Hector Banks shortly before Candi collapsed. He would have had to have been a skilled actor to have faked his drunkenness so well. "I don't think so."

Alex nodded. "Yeah, neither did we. Did you learn anything else from the Albrights?"

"He accompanied a woman out to a red hatchback car in his driveway and handed off a cardboard box while I was there," I said. Alex made a note of this in his ever-present notebook. "Brock was really tight-lipped. He clearly didn't want me there. And neither of them wanted to tell me anything about where I could find David. I know you've already interviewed him, but if you and Detective Reinhart are heading over to interview the parents, that might be a good question to start with."

"We're headed there later this afternoon, actually." He got up with his plate, and I watched to see if he was going to put back a fourth serving, but instead, he rinsed his plate and put it into the dishwasher.

"Let me know if you find out anything I couldn't," I told him, even though it seemed a ridiculous request. He was a police officer on a case, after all, and what was I?

When he turned from the dishes, he looked me over. I'd worn jeans and an argyle sweater this morning, as it had been quite chilly when Amber and I had left the house, but I suspected he wasn't concerned about my choice of wardrobe.

"You know you have to keep everything I've told you to yourself, right?" Alex asked.

I got it. He was trying so hard to get himself promoted within the department. Coming here and spilling everything he and Detective Reinhart had done so far on the Candi Banks murder case was most certainly not an item to be completed on their docket.

But I hoped one day Alex Martinez would trust me enough that he wouldn't have to ask.

"I won't say a word," I told him. "Think of me as a special consultant. And if Amber or I can come up with any other definite leads on who might have killed Candi Banks, you'll be the first to know."

Chapter Thirteen

AMBER SHOWED UP AT my door just after two, this time unannounced. I was still repacking leftovers from the picnic and handwashing dishes to return to church members.

She knocked, let herself in without waiting for me to answer, and started talking before she'd even reached the kitchen. "Seth was getting groceries for Mom, so he dropped me off on his way. Said he could pick me up in an hour, but I'll text him if you can drop me off later."

"I can," I told her. It wasn't like I had much else on my agenda.

"Good. Get your shoes on."

I looked down. She hadn't taken hers off. Hunch hadn't wasted any time in dragging his cast over to plant himself at her feet, and he sniffed her shoes as if interested in the unusual practice as well, as Cooper and I hadn't been in a habit of wearing our shoes in our new house.

Then again, my cat was more likely getting a historical account of the entire day solely through the scent of her shoes. But I wasn't a cat with an acute sense of smell and a keen discernment for all things mysterious, so I had to come out and ask. "Where are we going?"

"Honeysuckle Grove Rod and Gun Club. I called to see if Hector Banks was a member."

"And he is?" I asked, slinging the wet dish towel over the oven handle and then heading for the front door.

"Not only is he a member, but he shoots there every afternoon."

~~~

I'd never been much of a fan of guns.

As Amber and I got out of the Jeep and a shot echoed through the nearby air, it made me startle. Amber-the-Fearless grabbed my arm and pulled me toward the cedar pillars that marked the entrance to the gun club.

We entered into a small room that looked like a gun shop. At least a dozen rifles hung on the wall behind a glass counter filled with various types of bullets. Back when I used to help research Cooper's novels, I probably could have told you which bullets were made for which guns, but those sorts of details went in one ear and out the other with me now.

A man with an unkempt red beard, who looked like he belonged on Duck Dynasty, greeted us. "What can I do y'all for?"

I surveyed the small room, looking for the preprepared excuse I should have come in with.

Yet again, Amber was one step ahead of me. "I just need to talk to my Uncle Hector for a minute."

Apparently, Amber wasn't above telling a few lies to get to the greater truth.

Duck Dynasty glanced to a side door, as though that was where Hector could be found, and then looked Amber up and down. "Hector Banks? You Candi's sister?" The man didn't show a hint of sadness, even though he seemed to know Candi, which made me suspect he hadn't heard about her death.

"Yup," Amber said, crossing her arms as though defying him to challenge her on it.

He wasn't the type to be intimidated. "Sure don't look alike, do ya?"

"You know Candi?" I asked, to try and break up this power battle. I turned to Amber. "You didn't tell me your sister comes here, Lacey."

Duck Dynasty looked between us. Then he answered me. "Sure, Candi comes in with Hector every couple weeks to shoot. The boys around here sure like her. If you ask me, she likes the attention."

So this guy definitely didn't know Candi was dead. I wondered, if Hector was here right now, why he wouldn't have told this guy. Then again, maybe Duck Dynasty's macho attitude made the hackles of more than just fifteen-year-old girls prick up.

"So can I go back and see him?" Amber asked.

Duck Dynasty shrugged and pushed a logbook across the counter. "Just need your John Henrys first."

Amber signed "Lacey Banks" in big loopy handwriting. I wasn't sure what to write, but figured writing

Mallory Beck wouldn't be the smartest move. The first name I could come up with was a combination of two names currently swimming in my head: Alexis Albright. I scrawled it messily, so it wouldn't be completely readable, and a second later, Duck Dynasty opened a gate that led us to the side door.

Right as we reached for the handle, another gunshot went off, this one louder than the one from the parking lot had been, and it practically made me jump out of my skin.

"Come on," Amber—aka Lacey— told me, as though she knew I needed the push.

Moments later, we were outside again, but now under a long, sheltered overhang, lined with free-standing mini tables that faced a large open field. Hector Banks wasn't hard to spot among the three men spread out along the firing range. The other two had long beards like their Duck Dynasty buddy, and while Hector was by no means clean-shaven, his three- or four-day facial growth looked more lazy than intentional.

Thankfully, the red-bearded man from the front counter hadn't followed us outside. Amber led the way to Hector. He wore the same kind of plaid shirt and dirty jeans he'd worn to his niece's wedding, and he was currently leaning down, trying to line up a shot.

A faded white line marked the area non-shooters were to stand behind. Amber stood right on the line with her arms crossed while Hector took his time lining up the shot. I covered my ears, but nevertheless, as always, when he finally took the shot, the loud bang sent my heart skittering. A paper target fluttered from the bullet half a mile into the field in the distance. I squinted, but couldn't tell from here how accurate Hector's shot had been.

He was no more than two feet in front of us and must have felt our presence because he glanced over his shoulder and then straightened away from the free-standing table he had been lining his gun up on.

"Yeah?" he said. He was quite the opposite, at least in appearance, of his very proper older brother, Candi's dad. "What do ya want?"

"To ask you a few questions. Go ahead and finish up." Amber motioned her chin toward the target in the open field. Her stalling told me she must be nervous, too. Either that, or like me, she thought it might be better for him to have emptied all of his bullets before we started grilling him about his niece's murder.

Then again, we should probably leave the grilling for Alex and Detective Reinhart. We were just here to gather intel, I told myself for the twentieth time.

Hector started to turn away, but then swung back to us, leaving his gun set up where it was. "This about Candi?"

Amber nodded. "Yeah. She was a friend of mine. I just want to know what happened."

Good play, Amber! I wondered if I could pass as Amber's mom, or maybe better to play the aunt—for some sort of "kinship" to Candi's uncle. But Hector barely even glanced my direction and didn't seem to care who I was.

Hector shook his head and looked genuinely in turmoil as he said, "I dunno, but the police are sayin' she wasn't stung by no bee. They're saying they found some kinda needle stuck in her back."

Detective Reinhart must have divulged the ambiguous nature of Candi's death. I couldn't help myself. I glanced at his rifle.

Hector didn't miss the inference. "I didn't poke her with no needle! I woulda never done nothin' to hurt Candi."

The two long-bearded men looked over with raised bushy eyebrows. There wasn't much that intimidated Amber, but Hector's loud and sudden voice did. She took a step back, and I figured it was my turn to ask a question.

"Isn't it true, though, that she didn't want you at her wedding?" My hair was up in a knot, as I'd been packing up food when Amber had come by, so I hoped he wouldn't recognize me from the park, where I'd worn my hair down around my shoulder.

Hector let out a humorless laugh. "What she didn't want was for me and her mom to get into it. If she didn't want anyone there, it was her mother. But a bride can't exactly say that, now can she?"

"And so it had nothing to do with the fact that you showed up drunk?"

I didn't know what I expected. Perhaps for my words to rile Hector up, but they seemed to have the opposite effect. He shrugged and said, "Candi knows—knew—I had to have a couple to be around Tobias and Ella."

I hadn't known the first names of Candi's parents, but now that Hector said them, I could recall Tobias kneeling in panic near Candi's unresponsive body and repeatedly calling his wife, Ella.

Hector grabbed his phone from his front jeans pocket. "You want proof?" he asked. In mere seconds, he had scrolled through his phone and held up a photo of Candi in this exact same shelter, goggles over her eyes, a giant smile enveloping her face. He swiped to another photo of her leaning over a gun, and then several more photos of her grinning in front of the local smoothie shop with a giant purple-and-green cup in her hand.

The other shooters had lost interest in us and had gone back to lining up their own shots. I braced myself for when I might hear another shot.

Hector continued to scroll through more photos. He certainly did seem to have a lot of happy photos of Candi on his phone. And we could question Duck Dynasty at the counter on our way out to see exactly how well Hector and Candi seemed to get along when they came in together.

Amber had another question. "If you didn't stick a poisoned needle into my friend, who did? Did her mom do this to her?" Amber crossed her arms again, her intimidation stance. I wasn't sure if it was actually working on Hector Banks, but he seemed to know how to talk to teens without being patronizing, I'd give him that.

"Nah." Hector shook his head. "The two could scream at each other at home and then vent their anger at either me or Lacey in order to look like the perfect mother/daughter in public.

But Ella wouldn't have it in her to kill nobody, no matter how mad she got."

"Speaking of Lacey," I said. "She didn't get on too well with Candi either, huh?"

Hector shrugged. "Lacey's got a chip on her shoulder, thought Candi always got the best of everything. Been that way for years. But she seemed to like David. From what Candi had told me, she was pushing for them to get married."

I squinted, thinking. Was Candi's younger, jealous sister trying to be magnanimous? Or was she planning out a very specific—and very tragic—wedding day for her sister?

"You want to look into somebody?" Hector said. "I'd look at that gold-digger groom of Candi's."

"David?" I asked.

Hector kept his eyes on Amber as he elaborated. "Kid comes from some low-rent family that doesn't want him havin' nothin' they can't grow in their own backyard garden. Made sense he wanted out."

"Well, why not just marry Candi, then?" Amber, as usual, was quick with her smart questions. "I never trusted David," she said, still playing the part of Candi's friend, "but why would he kill his meal ticket out of there? Or at the very least, why wouldn't he wait until *after* they were married to do it?"

"That I don't know," Hector said. He was definitely soberer here today than he had been at the wedding. I wondered if sobriety was a necessity at a gun range. It would make sense if it was. "But I do know Tobias was trying to talk Candi into a prenup, and she wouldn't take it to David. I also know David's trying to claim squatters rights in that house Tobias had put a down payment on for Candi and David."

Squatters rights? That was why David had been staying there, even though his parents wanted him back home.

"You know where this house of David and Candi's is?" Amber asked, her phone at the ready to take down the address. "I was out of town when they got it."

Even though the lies were getting less believable, Hector shrugged and rattled off an address on Franklin Avenue, not too far from the Bankses' fancy neighborhood.

"And where are you living right now?" I asked Hector.

He studied me for a few long seconds. It didn't make sense why I was asking, and search my brain as I might, I couldn't seem to come up with a reasonable explanation.

But thankfully Amber, as always, could. "Were you living in the same house as Candi when she died?"

Hector didn't hesitate to answer Amber. I got the impression he trusted teenagers a lot more than he trusted adults. "Me 'n Ella can't be in the same room for too long, so when she's around, I've been crashing on friends' couches or in my car sometimes, until I can get back on my feet. Candi was gonna let me move into the basement of her new place, but I don't think David's gonna be so generous."

"Anything else you can tell us about David Albright that we might not know?" Amber asked. "I wanted to go talk to him next." She had relaxed her stance. I could read in her posture that she no longer suspected Hector Banks of being guilty.

Hector chuckled. "Ask him about his parents' secrets. Ask him about their precious greenhouse."

This brought us back to a feud between the Bankses and the Albrights. Perhaps tracking down Troy Offenbach could wait for the moment.

Chapter Fourteen

DAVID ALBRIGHT ANSWERED THE door to the two-story house he'd been squatting in, holding a game controller in one hand and chomping on a Pop-Tart with the other. I almost had to do a double-take. Was this the same young man who had grown up with Brock and Braidsy Naturalist out in Farmland, USA?

"Hi!" I said. As usual, I hadn't done much to prepare any specific line of questioning, even if Amber and I had chattered on about David for the entire fifteen-minute drive to get here. I nudged her forward and said, "This was a friend of Candi's who just got back into town and heard about the tragedy." Amber was so much better than me at discreet questioning.

"Oh. Uh. Come in," David said around a mouthful of crumbs. His eyes opened wide, and I couldn't tell if he was surprised or trying to hide his grief. He wore sweatpants and a dirty gray T-shirt that looked like it had old tomato sauce smeared on it. His shaggy dark hair stuck up at all angles as though he hadn't seen the inside of a shower yet today, even though it was nearly four in the afternoon.

I couldn't get my head around the fact that Candi had broken up with Troy to date, and even marry, this guy who must be barely out of high school. If Candi was going to rush into getting married, I would've expected it to be with someone who looked like he could hold a job and make a rent payment. Not the guy who couldn't even keep track of his Pop-Tart crumbs.

The inside of David's entryway overflowed with a multitude of boxes. The boxes continued as David led us up the stairs and into what I imagined was supposed to be a living room. This room was a far cry from any typical living room, though. Splayed in the middle of the floor was a mattress covered in messy blankets. If not for the high-tech gaming chair with speakers in the headrest, I would've suspected David to have been in bed all day, which I supposed wouldn't have been an unusual expression of grief. A flat-screen TV with a paused video game encompassed most of the largest wall in the room, but other than that, the room was filled only with more boxes. Most of these ones were either gift-wrapped or partially unwrapped. I wasn't entirely sure why David had led us up here, as it didn't seem there was anywhere other than the gaming chair to sit.

"Looks like you've just moved in," I observed. And had been playing video games nonstop since your wife-to-be was killed. Amber hadn't launched in with any of her astute questions, so I figured I'd might as well open up with the obvious.

"Uh-huh," David said, and then shoved the rest of the Pop-Tart into his mouth.

"Wow, this is a lot of stuff. All yours?" I wasn't sure how else to ask if any of it was Candi's.

David looked almost like a lost child when he shook his head and said, "Most of it was hers. Then my groomsmen, who were really just friends of Candi's, dropped the gifts from the park off here." He rubbed the back of his neck. "Not sure what to do with it all. Don't really want to call her parents."

I wondered if he'd rather not call her parents because they were grieving or because they might find a way to kick him out. This kid didn't seem like much of a brilliant schemer, though.

I looked around again at all the boxes, piles and piles of them against every wall. Maybe he couldn't sue for half of Candi's money because the wedding ceremony hadn't actually happened, but I wondered if all this stuff could have been enough motive for David to kill his bride.

Amber pointed to the gaming chair. "Was that one of the gifts? Or was it Candi's?"

My forehead buckled. Gaming chairs were comfortable, but it seemed a strange wedding gift. Although, now that Amber asked, I was unable to picture such an item in the Albright farmhouse—unless maybe it had been a gift from the same grandmother who had given him the lava lamp.

But David nodded at Amber's question and looked down, as though sadness was momentarily overtaking him. When he looked back up, he pointed across the room at a large gift-wrapped box. "Yeah. That one was supposed to be Candi's. Not sure what to do with that now either."

Who on earth gave matching gaming chairs for a wedding gift? I had to know. "Well, who gave them to you? Maybe they could get a gift receipt."

David shrugged again. "Candi's Uncle Hector bought them. He knew it's what Candi wanted, but he picked 'em up off eBay and dropped 'em off here last week. I doubt he can get his money back. Heard he used his rent money to buy 'em, too. Besides, I don't really want to get rid of Candi's. They're kind of a pair, you know?" He looked down at his feet again pensively. "Not sure I want to set it up, though, either."

"Understandable." I nodded, wondering if we'd have to track Hector down again to ask him why using rent money to buy the new couple gaming chairs seemed like a good idea. Then again, he'd likely just say that he cared about his niece and wanted to get her whatever her heart desired.

David stared at the unopened gaming chair, pensive for several long seconds. When he spoke again, he turned to Amber and asked, "Were you at the wedding?" Maybe it was too much to hope that none of our questions would raise David's suspicions.

"Yeahhhh." Amber drew out the word and walked over to the front window, I suspected to buy time. She looked down at the driveway where I'd parked the Jeep. There had been no other vehicles in the driveway, and I wondered if David owned a car. I suspected not if he was only eighteen and didn't appear to be made of money.

"I was out of town with my parents and arrived a little late, after everything happened." Amber's voice wavered on the word "parents" and I wondered if it was the first time she'd used the word since her dad had died.

"We stopped by your family's farmhouse to drop off a casserole," I told David, mostly to take the focus away from Amber. "I suggested I could drop some food off for you, too, but they said you'd be moving back with them within a few days." If that was the case, did he plan to bring all of these boxes back to the tiny farmhouse? Again, I couldn't picture it.

But David seemed to become energized by my question. He swiped food wrappers off the floor, tossed them toward a wastebasket in the corner, and then fanned the crumpled blanket over the mattress, effectively making up the bed in one quick motion. "I may not be able to stay here forever, but I'm not moving back there. Not ever."

"No? It was that bad?" I looked at Amber. The subject of his parents had him clearly agitated.

David stared at me for a few long seconds and then looked away. "Doesn't matter. I'm not going back." He paced toward the window and gazed outside. "Hopefully, the Bankses'll let me stay here until I can get a job and find somewhere cheaper to live."

"That's some fancy greenhouse they had out back," Amber said, and that's when I remembered Hector mentioning this trigger point for David—not that he seemed to need any more trigger points. "I can't believe they keep a lock on it. They sure keep a lot of plants, huh?"

David scowled, turning from the window. "They showed *you* the greenhouse?"

Amber shrugged. "Not exactly. But I found it."

David's scowl softened. "Right, well, they don't let anyone inside there, not even me. You want to know what would be so bad about moving back with them? Try being kept on some farmland off the bus routes where you can't go anywhere or see anyone. Try having your parents whisper secrets around your own house and not even let you answer your own front door. If I hadn't met Candi at the farmer's market where my mom had me selling vegetables, if she hadn't been willing to pick me up and take *me* on our dates, I never woulda gotten outta there!"

I could feel David's embarrassment mixed with anger vibrating throughout the room around us. I hated to do it, but now was the time to strike with the most important question.

"And if anyone wanted Candi dead, who do you think it would be?"

My mind was suddenly on David's father, Brock Albright. What did he have locked in that secret black-plastic-covered greenhouse of his? And if he'd been so incredibly strict with his only prized son, what would he have done to someone who interfered with his parenting?

David's eyes shifted back and forth over my face as though it was the daily newspaper. He took a long time to ask, "You think someone did this to Candi on purpose?"

I didn't know how long this information would take to come out as an official statement from the police. If Hector already knew and liked to drink, it likely wouldn't take long to get out, at least unofficially.

I tilted my head and answered David's question with a question. "What if they did?"

David kept his continually shifting eyes on me. His jaw tightened. Then he studied the floor for several long seconds. The delay stretched the tension in the room like a taut rubber band. Finally, he said, "That ex of hers. His name's Troy Offen-somethin'." David kept his eyes narrowed at the floor as he recounted the details he knew about Troy. "When we first pulled up to the park in the limo and Mrs. Winters told us about the double-booking of the park, Candi freaked out. She said, 'If Troy can't have me, he wants to make sure no one can!'" Finally, David looked up at us. "Everybody in the wedding party heard her." He started pacing, raking his hands through his hair, practically frantic.

I looked at Amber. If this was true, the next item on our agenda was clearly to talk a confession out of Troy Offenbach.

"Would you be willing to tell the police what you just told us?" I pulled a notepad and pen from my purse and scrawled Alex's name and number onto it. I passed it to David, even though he still hadn't answered me. "If there was foul play involved with Candi's death, you'd want to know who did this, right?"

Finally, he nodded, but he still looked shell-shocked at the idea of Candi being murdered. David's answers weren't enough to clear his name from suspicion completely, but as far as I was concerned, Amber and I had more promising suspects to investigate.

Chapter Fifteen

ON THE DRIVE TO HONEYSUCKLE Grove Community Church, Amber called to check in with her brother, Seth, again. Her mom was medicating herself to get through her grief and might not notice if Amber disappeared for a week, but her brother looked out for her more and more with each passing day, and Amber seemed to appreciate it.

"Yeah, maybe an hour or two," she said into her phone.

Often, the only way I knew what was going on in Amber's overactive head was to eavesdrop in on her phone conversations. If she only planned to be gone another hour or two, it seemed finding and interviewing Troy Offenbach was likely the last item on our agenda today.

"Hey, do you know a girl named Lacey Banks?" she asked into her cell phone. It wouldn't have occurred to me to ask Amber's brother this, but it made sense. They were close to the same age. "Uh-huh. Oh, yeah? What about a guy named David Albright?" I suspected he had been homeschooled and wasn't all that socially connected in Honeysuckle Grove, so it surprised me when Amber said, "Oh, really?" like something had surprised her. I wished she'd put it on speaker, but instead, I tapped my fingers on the steering wheel impatiently until she hung up.

"What did you find out about Lacey?" I hadn't given Amber all of the details Alex had passed along— confidentiality, and all—but I had

225

mentioned Lacey had been spotted laughing with friends.

"She was a year ahead of Seth in school, graduated last year, and he said he only knew her by reputation."

"What kind of reputation?"

Amber laughed. "Apparently she was a bit of a pothead, known for her money and her stupidity. Paid people gobs of money to write all of her essays and even take her exams. She'd been caught more than once, and if rumors were correct, the only reason she graduated was because of the huge donations her parents made to the school's building fund." Amber looked at me with a raised eyebrow. "This doesn't sound like the type of girl who could orchestrate or take part in a very public murder, no matter how much she hated her sister."

She might be right. "And David Albright? Did your brother know him?"

She shook her head. "No, but he knew the last name. Said everyone he knew who bought drugs got them from some guy named Albright."

With only one Albright in the local phone book, I was willing to bet I'd been correct about Brock Albright conducting a grow-op in the greenhouse in his backyard. I didn't have time to think more about this, though, as I pulled into the church parking lot. It was five on the nose, closing time. Penny Lismore was just pulling her key from the office door and turned for the lone car in the parking lot, not noticing my Jeep near the curb of the main sanctuary.

I jumped out of the Jeep on one side, and Amber wasn't far behind me on the other.

"Penny! Penny, can I speak to you for a moment?" I jogged over, glad to have Amber with me, if for no other reason that I often chose sneakers for my footwear when we went out together.

Penny had reached her car already, a small lime-green Datsun that looked striking against her bright orange hair. She stopped and turned my way. "Hi. What can I do for you?" Her question was wary. I got the feeling people asking her for help after hours wasn't exactly an unusual occurrence.

"We were wondering if Troy Offenbach, the church treasurer, was still here?" I motioned to the church office, even though it seemed unlikely, as there were no other cars and the interior lights all appeared to be out.

Penny shook her head. "I'm afraid not." Her tone didn't invite conversation, but thankfully, Amber wasn't deterred.

"But he did come in today, right?"

Penny looked between Amber and me like she didn't know who to answer. She settled her gaze somewhere in between us. "Sure, he was in, but he leaves early on Mondays.

He's still working on his degree at the college and has a class at five."

"An accounting class?" I asked.

Penny shrugged. "I suppose so."

"How did he seem today? He was pretty broken up yesterday about the incident at the park, right? I understand he knew the bride?"

Penny nodded and looked down at the pavement in front of her solemnly. "Yes. I still can't believe what happened, but Troy certainly felt it more than the rest of us. He broke down at the copier today, said it was only three months ago that they had been dating. I feel awful for him."

I looked to Amber, a wave of sadness coming over me as well. But she looked as stoic and in control as always. I supposed that was what happened when you found out your dad was murdered by someone you'd have never suspected in a million years. Other people's tragedies probably didn't seem quite as tragic after that.

But my bleeding heart didn't stop with Troy. I had to ask after our wounded pastor as well. "And Pastor Jeff? I don't suppose he was here today, but have you heard if he's out of the hospital?"

Penny sighed and looked up at us, but her countenance didn't appear much brighter. "They're keeping him one more night, just to be sure the toxin has been cleared from his system. I'm headed there now."

"Well, give him our best, will you?" I said, taking a step back so she could go. There was nothing more to learn from Penny Lismore. I was quite certain she wasn't lying about Troy's outburst earlier today, so there were three possible conclusions I could draw from that:

One. Troy Offenbach killed Candi but was a really good actor.

Two. He'd killed Candi and had experienced a deep wave of remorse about it today.

Three. He was innocent and was heartbroken that she'd died.

I wanted to believe the third option, but then again, I tended to want to believe that of everyone.

"Should I take you home?" I asked Amber, but I knew her answer before I'd even asked the question.

"No. You should take me to Honeysuckle Grove Community College. We're going to talk to Troy."

Chapter Sixteen

I FIGURED WE HAD LOTS of time before we could track down Troy, and so I did a drive-thru run on our way over to the community college. Even if Troy's class was only an hour, it wouldn't let out before six.

Amber took a bite of her burger and scowled. "Guess I haven't had fast-food since I've been cooking with you. This is gross."

"You're welcome," I said with a smirk. But I understood what she meant. I wasn't a big fan of fast-food myself, although I found when I was working through a mystery, my brain didn't seem to have room for everything, so food tended to lose its variances—unless something struck me as particularly awesome, like the eggplant parmesan I'd had at lunch.

As I pulled into the college's parking lot, I went over the three possibilities again. "So he's a good actor, he's feeling guilty, or he's innocent. How do we find out which?"

Amber finished chewing and swallowed before answering. "I think we need to start with how to find his classroom." She looked across the sprawling building. The parking lot was about half-full, which meant there were a good number of evening classes going on today.

"Yeah, you're right. I doubt the college office is open after five, but I still want to be ready with some good questions this time."

Amber shrugged, shoving another bite into her mouth. The speed at which she inhaled her burger indicated she couldn't think it was *that* awful. I took my first nibble, but as usual, I wasn't hungry so much as needing to do something with my hands. Cooking or kneading bread would've been preferable.

Finally, Amber swallowed again and rattled off questions as though they came as naturally to her as breathing. "How'd he and Candi break up? Was he angry about it? Was he angry at her? Why did he only book one shelter at the park for the church? Did he know Candi's wedding was going to be held on the same day at the same park? Why did he have the park mail him the bill directly, instead of to the church?"

When the questions came all in a row like that, they made Troy Offenbach seem guilty. "Maybe I should call Alex," I suggested.

Amber raised her eyebrows and drilled her fifteen-year-old fearless gaze into me. "Maybe I should have brought your cat along instead. He'd have the nerve to do a little fact-checking before we bring the police into it."

She was right. I was scared. What if this was a murderer we were about to confront? Then again, we were in a public place. Chances were good that Troy wouldn't be carrying around a toy gun loaded with poisoned needles to his college classes. And it really would be good to go back to Alex with something more substantial than theories.

"You're right," I told her. I could prove myself at least as helpful as my three-legged ornery cat. "Let's go and see if we can find the accounting wing."

It turned out the community college's board of directions at the front entrance made this part of things easy. Business classes were to the right, in the "E" wing. We headed that way.

"It's pretty nice that the church is letting Troy work as treasurer, even though he hasn't finished his degree," Amber said as we walked. Less than a dozen people passed us as we wove down long hallways and around corners, following other signage toward Wing E. "My career ed. teacher from last year said to break into jobs in business you almost always needed a bachelor's degree or even a master's."

This didn't surprise me if Pastor Jeff had done the hiring. He would most certainly want to help a young person out if it was within his power. "I just hope he didn't throw away a great opportunity," I said, still wanting to believe in Troy's innocence, despite Amber's long list of accusatory questions for him.

I'd barely finished my sentence when Amber threw an arm out in front of my chest to stop me. She pointed two fingers at her wide eyes and then straight ahead, where not fifty feet in front of us, a man who looked like Troy Offenbach, with trim blond hair and long legs, sat alone on a bench with his head between his hands.

Amber and I took about three seconds to look at each other, survey the situation, and then forge ahead.

I still wasn't entirely sure it was him, so when we got about ten feet away and he still hadn't looked up, I said, "Troy?"

Slowly, he lifted his head from his hands to reveal red and swollen eyes behind his wire-rimmed glasses. It was him. He pulled off his glasses to wipe them on his tan-colored dress shirt and then replaced them. I looked around at this empty hallway in Wing E. If he was still acting, I wasn't sure for whose benefit.

"We're sorry to bother you," I said quickly because all of a sudden, I was afraid of Amber taking over with her blunt and badgering questions. "But are you okay?"

Troy looked between me and Amber, and then took a deep breath. "Oh, yes. I'm—" His words started out stoic, like he was putting on a front of having it all together when he recognized us, but his voice broke on the last word, and he looked down at his lap, blinking fast, unable to finish his sentence.

It was my first inclination to slide onto the bench and wrap an arm around him, but Amber spoke up, reminding me of why we were here. "I knew Candi and her sister, Lacey, from school. I just can't even believe what happened. You and Candi used to date, right?" Amber didn't drum up any tears with her words, but she did exude more compassion than I would've expected.

Troy's forehead creased toward Amber. "You were friends with Candi?"

Amber forced a sad smile in way of an answer.

He only nodded. "So you must have been there for the wedding that day?"

"I was at the park when she collapsed, yeah." She impressed me, answering so seamlessly without any out-and-out lies.

"I was surprised to see the church picnic was going to be at the same park. It didn't seem like it would've been big enough."

I was quite certain I didn't imagine Troy's eyes flitting away from me for half a second on that statement. His reaction made me push on with, "Did you know there was a wedding scheduled when you booked the park for the church?"

The bottom rims of his eyes collected water, and again the three options raced through my brain: actor, guilt-ridden, or innocent?

Troy looked down. His answer was barely audible when he said, "I...yeah."

"Were you still in love with Candi?" Amber's question shocked me. It hadn't been on her list, but as usual, my astute young friend seemed to know how to get to the heart of the matter.

Troy nodded down at the floor.

Amber's voice became surprisingly gentle as she said, "And you hoped she wouldn't go through with the wedding if the park wasn't perfect? Or when she saw you there?"

Troy removed his glasses again to wipe his eyes. I felt awful for him. This wasn't the work of an actor, unless he was well beyond Al Pacino in skill and training. He was either severely guilt-ridden or innocent, although now I suspected that even if he was innocent of killing Candi, he still felt guilty for double-booking the park, if that was what led to her death.

"Are you done your class already?" I asked, feeling the need to give both of us a reprieve from these heavy emotions.

Troy heaved in a breath and let it out in a sigh. "I couldn't bring myself to go. This here, this bench, it's where Candi and I met. She was taking a class in cosmetic management. She wanted to own her own spa one day." He choked through the words to get them out.

It was all starting to make sense now. Troy had deeply cared about Candi and was willing to ruin her wedding to show her how much.

"What about David, her groom?" I hated to ask this, but it had to be done. "They must have been madly in love to have such a whirlwind relationship and quick wedding, right?"

Troy's face hardened as he replaced his glasses and looked up at me. "Candi wasn't in love with him. She was in love with her childhood, the lack of responsibility she'd had before her mom forced her to go to college. She dropped out right after she met him, did you know that? She could have been so much more, and David Albright was going to ruin her life!"

"And you would have done anything to stop it?" Amber prodded more bluntly than I would've.

"I would have broken up their wedding, yeah. Her mom would have, too." He popped off the bench, and it made me realize how tall he was as he loomed over us. "I'd never have done anything if I thought she'd get hurt, though." A new round of tears rimmed his eyes. "Not anything," he said.

I wanted to believe him. Amber, however, clearly wasn't there yet. At least her questions were getting gentler as she asked, "Why did you and Candi break up? Was it because of David?"

That seemed obvious to me, from everything Troy had told us so far, but surprisingly, he shook his head. "It was because of the baby." His words were so choked, I could barely make them out.

I had to confirm what he was saying. "Candi Banks was pregnant?" That was certainly something an autopsy could confirm, although I wasn't certain if it would prove anything about her murder, even if it was true.

But Troy shook his head. "It was an accident. She wasn't ready to grow up so fast, but I told her we could handle it. She could finish out the school year, we could get married and save for a home, even if her parents got angry about the pregnancy and wouldn't help us get one. I told her it might be tight, but my job at the church could support us. But within a week, she had aborted it and started dating a lowlife with no aspirations, zero job experience, and she blamed not wanting to see me as the reason she'd dropped out of school. She never did tell anyone about the baby." His bitter words made me realize again how different the two young men were.

"So Mrs. Banks was in on it with you? On breaking up the wedding?" I said to clarify.

He nodded. "First, we teamed up to try and get her back in school, but when that didn't work, I had an idea to double-book the park. Mrs. Banks kept telling Candi she deserved the perfect wedding, and not to accept anything less."

Troy's whole countenance was mixed between anger and hardness and crumpled emotion. Thankfully, Amber seemed to agree that this awful interview was over. She took a step backward.

I wanted to give Troy a hug, but thankfully caught myself, realizing that would be highly inappropriate. "I'm so sorry for your loss." The words—the unhelpful trite ones I swore I'd never say to another person after Cooper's death—launched out of my mouth without my permission.

Thankfully, Amber was much better at this than me. "Anyone could see Candi didn't love David. I'm sure she really loved you, too."

And as Troy Offenbach's countenance morphed into pure gratitude, Amber and I decided to leave him alone.

Chapter Seventeen

I WAS BEAT, AND FROM the silence in the Jeep, Amber was, too. Without discussing it, I headed for her family's mansion and pulled into her driveway. I was most certainly not interested in cooking tonight, and besides, Amber had her first day of tenth grade tomorrow. I'd be a cruel excuse for an adult figure if I kept her with me just to fill some insatiable need for company.

"Text me when you're done with school tomorrow," I told her. "Let me know how it goes."

Even though Amber and I had barely spoken about her school life, I'd gotten the impression she wasn't looking forward to it. She didn't seem to have good friends of her own age that she could have a heart-to-heart with about what had happened to her dad.

I was it. And if I were being honest, it made me grateful. She was pretty much it for friends I could talk to about losing Cooper as well.

Amber got out wordlessly and waved on her way to her front door.

I backed out of her driveway and headed away from her house, feeling loneliness overtake me with each yard I moved away from her. There was always Hunch, I told myself. A cat who didn't have an ounce of friendliness toward me was a poor consolation for my bright-eyed teenage friend, but at least it was something.

At the bottom of the hill from Amber's house, though, I was about to pass the local hospital and made a split-second decision to turn in. Penny indicated Pastor Jeff was just being kept overnight as a precaution, but I still couldn't help wanting to see him alive and breathing with my own eyes.

Then again, maybe it was simply that darn insatiable need for company.

Whatever the case, the nurse's station was quick to direct me to his room. Apparently, well-meaning folks from the church had been visiting him all day. I felt bad for being yet another of these folks. But not badly enough to turn around and go home. I knocked with two knuckles on the door I'd been directed to.

Emily's voice called a whispered, "Come in."

I nudged through the door and peeked around the curtain to find a sleeping Pastor Jeff. He normally had such a booming authoritative presence, it was odd to see him lying still and breathing evenly.

I turned to Emily on the chair beside him. Dark skin encircled her eyes. "How's he doing?" I asked softly.

"Good." Despite her obvious exhaustion, she launched out of her chair at seeing me and held out a hand toward it.

There was no way on God's green earth I was going to take her chair after the days she'd had, but I was certain she'd insist, so I waved a hand at the chair and told a half-truth. "I've been sitting all day. Please, you go ahead."

Thankfully, she didn't fight me on it.

"I hear they're keeping him an extra day as a precaution?" I whispered.

She nodded. "They gave him another full dose of the antidote this afternoon." She held up a small silver packet from his tray table, where another dozen silver packets lay. "They thought he should stay here for a full forty-eight hours, just in case it didn't completely clear his symptoms. It's basically just an H2 blocker called Nizatidine combined with a specific antacid—one with magnesium hydroxide. The doctor said it was the first line of defense, and it almost always worked as an antidote if they caught it quickly enough when patients came into the emergency room with symptoms of this particular wild plant poisoning." She looked down at the packet. "They said I could take a few of these home. If we had any concerns, he could just empty a packet under his tongue for quick absorption and then head straight to the hospital."

"Would you mind if I took a packet with me?" I asked. "I don't know if it would help discover anything about Candi's murder, but if the doctor hasn't already passed this antidote along to the forensics lab, I could give it to my police friend, just in case." I was probably reaching, trying to find anything at all helpful to do, but I couldn't seem to stop myself.

Emily Hawthorne grabbed two packets from the table and passed them over. She quirked up a smile with one side of her mouth, like she was too tired to lift both sides. "We'd be grateful if you can find out anything about that horrible tragedy. The family must be going out of their mind."

I opened my mouth to tell them it was Troy that seemed to be going out of his mind about Candi's death, but then I shut it. He could tell them more about his heartache when he was ready.

As I pulled out my phone and sent Alex a quick text, she added, "And thank you, Mallory. I've heard you've been getting in touch with people from the church about their dishes from the potluck. It's so nice to not have to concern ourselves with that."

I couldn't even imagine the church's pastor and his wife worrying about leftover dishes, even if he wasn't in the hospital. But knowing these two and their serving hearts, it seemed quite likely that they normally *did* do all these things themselves.

As I leaned in to give Emily a hug goodbye and then headed for the door, I vowed to be more helpful to both of them in the future.

Driving for home, I felt just as lonely as I had when I'd dropped Amber at her place. Alex still hadn't texted me back, and I doubted he was still at the police station this late.

Because I didn't want Detective Reinhart to somehow get the credit for turning the antidote into forensics, even if it was only a specific kind of H2 blocker/antacid combo, I was determined to hang onto it until I connected with Alex directly. If he told me they were already two—or more likely ten—steps ahead of me, so be it, but until then, I curled them up and

252

tucked them into the small pen loop of my cell phone case so I wouldn't lose them.

I pulled into my driveway and checked my phone again, but there was still no response. I sighed out a long breath and headed for the house.

Hunch, surprisingly, greeted me at the door. I hated to admit it, but that cat, if only he'd be nice to me, was exactly what I needed right now.

"Wait until I tell you about the day I had investigating," I said, just to keep his attention as I slipped out of my shoes. As I said the words, though, I realized they were true. I *did* have a lot to tell Hunch. "Come on. Let's go curl up on the couch, and I'll tell you everything."

Shock of my life—Hunch stayed right on my heels as I took a few steps toward the living room. Because he struggled with moving around with his cast, I bent down with my arms out to offer to carry him, and the second shock of my life came when he walked right into them.

Twenty minutes later, I had spelled out most of my afternoon and evening. Hunch knew about Alex coming by at lunch today—at least as well as a cat could know about things in the human world—so instead, I delved into our interview with gun-happy Uncle Hector, David Albright and his matching gaming chairs, Troy Offenbach and his extreme grief over losing a baby, losing Candi to David, and then losing Candi altogether, and then my final stop at the hospital, where I picked up an antidote to pass along to the police.

Hunch sat on my lap, purring and looking me straight in the eye, as if he were hearing and understanding every word. I was petting my cat's soft fur with one hand and studying one of the H2 blocker/antacid packets with the other when my phone rang. Alex Martinez's name appeared on the display, along with the time, which was after 11:00 p.m. I quickly replaced the silver packet and answered.

"Sorry to call so late," he said in way of a hello. "I just got your message now. Steve brought me along on a stakeout for the night so we can discuss the case. It's been a crazy day."

"Oh, yeah? Anything new you can share?"

Alex cleared his throat. "You're on speakerphone. I filled Steve in on what you'd found out at the Albrights'."

I opened my mouth, but I didn't know what to say. Was Detective Reinhart upset that I'd been running around, conducting my own mini-investigation?

But he spoke next and cleared it up for me. "When we went over to question them, Brock Albright didn't even let us in the door. Told us to come back with a warrant."

As Hunch kneaded my lap and mewled, I, with a crazy overestimation of my cat, decided to put my phone on speakerphone as well. "Amber said her brother knew of a drug dealer in town who goes by the name of Albright. Do you think that's why he's so secretive? Is that where you're staking out?"

Alex answered me. "No, the stakeout is for another case. Anyway, we hope to have a warrant and get back there to check out the house and greenhouse by the weekend."

The weekend was still four days away.

"*If* we can find the time to get over there again," Detective Reinhart put in. "Between finding a few hours to sleep, following up on all the leads on the Hackendale case, and meeting with forensics, it might be next week."

I opened my mouth to offer my help, but closed it before anything could come out. Of course, they wouldn't want, nor would they ever ask for, my help. Instead, I hung on the word "forensics" and asked, "Did they determine a definite cause of death for Candi Banks? Or any matching fingerprints?"

"Yeah," Detective Reinhart told me and again dispelled the myth that I might be prying too hard for information. "The fact that the epinephrine had seemingly compounded the toxin's effect led the ER doctor to suggest possible strychnine poisoning, but that didn't add up when considering how fast-acting it had been. I mentioned that Jeff Hawthorne's managing doctor had suggested a different strain of plant substance it could have been derived from. Something called sciadotenia toxifera, a fast-acting vesicant. Our lab techs weren't familiar, but once we passed along the name from the doctor, they were able to look into the chemical compounds further. A full toxicology report could take weeks, though."

I fiddled with one of the silver packets again. I had wanted to get this information to Alex first, but I couldn't knowingly keep information from the police. "I was just at the hospital, and apparently, Pastor Jeff's treating doctor gave him some H2-blockers combined with an antacid for him to take home in case of furthering symptoms. I took a couple of packets with me in case they could be helpful in your forensics lab."

"Did you hear if they've gotten that yet, Alex?" Detective Reinhart asked.

Papers rustled through the phone, and a few seconds later, Alex said, "Um, I'm not sure..."

Great. My efforts to help Alex look good in the department's eyes had backfired

"Why don't you pick it up from her first thing in the morning when we're done here," Detective Reinhart said, "and drop it off at forensics? Looking at the combination under a microscope may help them understand the molecular structure better, and maybe help us figure out better who might have access to such a toxin."

Alex agreed, and I told him I'd be up early and would be happy to deliver it to him if it was easier.

"Did you get a chance to interview Lacey Banks? Or Hector?" After so much freely given information, I was now spouting my own interrogation questions as though I were part of the police force.

"We still haven't connected with Hector," Detective Reinhart said, "but the Bankses were cooperative when we went over to question Lacey. Mr. Banks assured us that if foul play was involved in Candi's death, they would do anything they could to help bring the guilty parties to justice."

So they had clearly informed Candi's parents of the homicide nature of the case. "And did Lacey's interview reveal anything helpful?"

"Unfortunately, not much beyond her hostile feelings toward her sister. Apparently, Candi always seemed to be favored by everything from teachers to the local press. We had to grill her a little, but we got it out of her that she was excited for the wedding, even while her mother was trying to delay or even stop it because she knew that once Candi was attached to a lowlife like David Albright, the press wouldn't want anything to do with her. In fact, she had expected that her wedding day would have been her last day in the limelight." Detective Reinhart sighed. "Upon questioning Lacey about her sister's death, she simply told us, 'Why would I have killed her? Now she'll be the talk of the town for at least another month.'"

"Wow, pretty coldhearted," I said.

"Yes, but I'm quite certain she's not the sociopath we're looking for in this case."

After Detective Reinhart had been so forthcoming with all of their information, I felt no reason to hide anything I had uncovered, especially if it could help. "Actually, Amber and I tracked down Hector Banks earlier today."

"Really? Where?" Alex and Detective Reinhart asked at the same time.

"We found him at the local gun range. Apparently, he goes there every day." I went on to explain how close he and Candi had been, the photos on his phone, and the time of day they'd be likely to track him down there. Then I told them about our conversation with Troy Offenbach.

"Yes, we got to him earlier today as well, but we hadn't heard about

Candi's mother being against the wedding until Lacey told us that part," Detective Reinhart said. "You clearly have a knack for hunting down suspects and asking the right questions, Mallory. It's always helpful to have someone who was on scene of a murder and can give us a better understanding of the events. I'll be sure to mark you down as a special consultant on this one."

I felt myself flush. "Well, any way I can help, I'm happy to, especially when it sounds like your detective unit has too much on its plate."

Detective Reinhart chuckled. "You can say that again."

"So I'll be over first thing," Alex said, "and we'll see if forensics can figure out anything else useful about this South African plant toxin."

After that, we all said goodbye. As I hung up, I was glad to finally have some motivation to go to bed. Otherwise, I'd likely spend the entire night retelling my stories to Hunch in order to keep him by my side.

I picked him up to carry him upstairs to the bedroom. Even on the days he hated me most, he at least kept Cooper's side of the bed warm, but tonight, as I carried him in that direction, he squirmed and pulled to get out of my arms.

"Hunch, it's bedtime!" I told him. Sometimes I thought the cat understood more words in the English language than I did. Other times, like this, I suspected he didn't comprehend a single one.

He dug his claws into my arm, and while I wasn't in the habit of throwing my cast-clad cat, I couldn't help myself. "Ow! What was that for?"

I ran a thumb over my stinging arm, and a streak of blood appeared. Stupid cat! I'd gone out and bought him a second litter box as well as food and water bowls after he'd been fitted for his cast, so he'd never feel imprisoned by the stairs. I always took him upstairs last thing at night and brought him back down first thing in the morning. So what was this cat's problem?

I looked away from my stinging arm to see Hunch nipping at the leaves of my spider plant in the corner. I let out an aggravated sigh and strode toward him. "Come on, Hunch. It's time for bed."

One more try, and I was leaving him down here for the night. I'd taken good care of Cooper's cat since my late husband's death as an honor to Cooper, but Hunch had never drawn blood before.

He looked up and actually growled at me.

I squinted, wondering if my cat had gone rabid in the last two minutes. He'd been so friendly while sitting on my lap and listening to my investigation stories and the conversation with the police officers.

He took another nip at the plant and looked back at me. That's when I clued in that he was trying to tell me something.

My thumb had been absently running over the antidote packet alongside my cell phone since I'd hung up from Alex's call. I blinked as a revelation was trying very hard to connect in my brain. The cat. The spider plant. The H2-blocker/antacid antidote.

The spider plant. My cat's unusual reaction to a plant...

All at once, it hit me: the Albright's greenhouse!

If the poison that killed Candi and almost took out Pastor Jeff had come from an unusual plant...where better to look for such a plant than in someone's private locked greenhouse?

Chapter Eighteen

HUNCH WOULDN'T LET ME go to bed after I finally got "Greenhouse!" out of our cat and mouse (or cat and human, in this case) game of charades. Of course, he wouldn't. But if I were being honest, the adrenaline that rushed through my veins with this new revelation wouldn't have let me sleep regardless.

I googled sciadotenia toxifera under a number of different spellings until I finally found the green-leafed plant with tiny yellow berries. It didn't inform me of much beyond what I already knew: It was a rare wild-growing poisonous plant, native to the forests of South Africa.

I went over all the information I had with Hunch again. I was no longer suspicious of Troy Offenbach or Hector Banks. And it sounded as though Detective Reinhart had cleared Lacey Banks from suspicion.

I clicked over to my phone icon and dialed Alex's number. It rang four times and then went to voicemail. Clearly, they were too busy on their stakeout to answer the phone. I didn't know any details of their other case, but I couldn't help picturing them with guns drawn, rushing into some rundown drug house or back alley, like I'd seen on TV stakeouts.

I nibbled my lip, hoping they were both okay. When Alex's voicemail beeped, I rattled off a message in little more than a whisper, feeling as if someone on the other end might hear me, and I could somehow blow their cover. "Alex! I just thought about it. What if Brock Albright is growing this rare South African toxic plant in his greenhouse? Amber stuck her gum into the lock of the gate yesterday, so I was thinking...if they're thinking you're going to come back with a warrant, maybe someone should look into what's in there before Brock can hide it away? I'm not sure about getting past the greenhouse lock, but I don't know, I feel like someone should get over there and check it out before it's too late. Get back to me when you can and let me know what you think."

Hunch and I both paced my living room for a full fifteen minutes, waiting for Alex to call back. Then a half hour. The words "special consultant" kept rattling around in my brain, egging me on, not to mention my increasingly-agitated feline friend's growls. Finally, I headed upstairs and pulled on a pair of black leggings and my darkest gray hoodie. I was tempted to text Amber and ask her to come along, but I reminded myself again and again that it was her first day of school tomorrow. Besides, I wasn't about to purposely drag a teenager into a dangerous situation.

Not that this was dangerous. I didn't plan to interrupt anyone's life or even let a single person know I was there. It was a fact-finding mission, I told myself for the twentieth time. Nothing more.

If I could get into the backyard and anything inside looked the least bit like the plant I'd found on the Internet, I'd tell Alex right away, and he could put a rush on that search warrant to investigate first thing in the morning—hopefully before the Albrights were any the wiser and could hide any incriminating evidence.

"If there are any signs that the Albrights might still be awake or that they have any kind of alarm system on that greenhouse, I'm out of there," I told Hunch. "No matter what you think."

Thankfully, he didn't growl or argue with me this time. I brought him downstairs to wait for me there, but as I slipped into some black sneakers, he meowed against the edge of the front door.

"You can't come," I told him, even though I kind of did want his company. "You can barely walk."

But when he mewled a frustrated meow at me again, even though I knew it was stupid, I picked the cat up in my arms and headed out the door.

"You can wait in the car," I told him.

I took the Prius, a hybrid that rode much quieter than Cooper's Jeep. Hunch sat with his cast awkwardly stretched out, but nevertheless upright at attention, as was becoming his habit whenever I brought him along on an investigation.

As I drove out of the center of town toward Honeysuckle Grove farmland, the streetlights came fewer and farther between. When I finally turned down Coventry Road, where the Albrights lived, everything seemed dark and quiet. The farm before their house had one light above its barn, but it only illuminated a small circle in front of it. Otherwise, the only light came from the moon as it moved in and out of cloud covering.

I pulled over onto the shoulder a few feet past the lit barn and well before the Albright farmhouse. It would be a bit of a walk to get to the greenhouse, but better too far away than too close.

"You're going to be stuck in here a while," I told Hunch. I was tempted to remind him not to pee in my car, but I realized before it left my mouth that Hunch was either much too responsible to let such an infantile occurrence happen or much too feline to understand my instructions. In eight and a half months, I hadn't discovered which was truer, so what made me think I'd have any real revelations about it tonight?

I picked through the small toolkit I'd brought along, shoving bits and pieces into my hoodie pockets. A tiny screwdriver here, a paperclip and hair clip there. I reached for the glove compartment, flipped it open, and slapped my hand around. My flashlight. Had I left it somewhere while investigating Dan Montrose's death?

No matter, I decided. The flashlight on my phone would work in a pinch, even if it was overly bright. I'd use it sparingly and only when out of view of any of the farmhouse windows. I grabbed my cell phone from the console to get the flashlight app open, but as soon as I flicked it on, I saw Alex had returned my call and left a voicemail, but my phone only had five percent of its battery life left. Usually, it was plugged in beside my bed by this time at night.

I sighed. This was going to be a super fast fact-checking mission after all, and I'd have to call Alex back when I could get back to the phone charger in my car, or I wouldn't have any flashlight at all to work with.

I got out of the Prius and closed the door silently. I'd do my best to navigate my way by moonlight alone as much as possible, only using my phone light when I absolutely needed it. Thankfully, traffic was thin on these farm roads at the best of times, and there were no cars at this time of night, so at least walking the long stretch of road to the Albright farmhouse was a breeze, even in the dark.

Once I could make out the frame of the Albright farmhouse, I decided it was time to leave the easy terrain of the road and wade through the thigh-high grass. I suspected, from the unkempt area, they didn't use this path often. I took each step slowly, ensuring I had solid footing before moving on. Maybe I should've brought one of Hunch's litter boxes in the car, I thought absently as I took another step, because at this rate, getting to the greenhouse and back to the Prius could well take me all night.

I paused and squinted around me, trying to get my bearings, even though a cloud had momentarily shielded the moon and it seemed much darker. The light from the neighboring barn in the distance gave me some sort of spatial awareness. I decided on moving closer to the farmhouse, close enough to run my hand along it. That would help me keep my bearings.

By the time I made it to the farmhouse, my leggings and shoes were soaked from dew. I shivered and told myself I had to be almost at the fence. It was a tiny farmhouse, and Amber had said the greenhouse was right behind it.

Just then, my hand hit something flat in front of me. Running a hand along the worn board, I immediately got a sliver, but I could tell this was definitely the fence in front of me. My hand gently led my way sideways until I found the small latch of the gate. It was a thumb-press latch. It wouldn't press, and I could find the lock above it by feel. But I gave the ten-foot gate a little nudge, and sure enough, Amber's gum must have still been in the strike plate because it moved forward.

I tiptoed through quietly, looking around me in the darkness to make sure nothing and no one had been disturbed. When I got to the back corner of the farmhouse, thankfully the moon had made a reappearance to help me along. Moonlight glinted off the black plastic of the greenhouse, and I could make out its large arched form. In fact, while not quite as tall, the oblong greenhouse seemed to cover much more land than the small farmhouse in front of it. The thing was huge!

I was so caught up in admiring the size of it and tiptoeing toward it, I was being less careful with each of my steps and paused when my foot squished into something soft.

I pulled out my phone, running my hand along its side to find the On button, but that's when I realized the packets of antidote were still curled into the penholder of my phone case. *Shoot.* I should have left those in the car, or better yet, at home. If I lost it out here in the overgrown grass, Alex would likely have to miss out on any sleep he could get in order to make a special trip to the hospital.

I pulled the packets from the pen loop and went to tuck it into my shoe, but as I flicked my flashlight on, just for a second, the squishy thing I'd stepped on came into view. I jumped back and tried my best to quell my scream with a hand over my mouth.

A dead rat.

It took me several seconds to regain my breath. Flies buzzed around the area, and I wondered if there were other dead—or alive—vermin nearby. Thankfully, I hadn't dropped the little silver packets because there was a zero percent chance I was going to get on my hands and knees in the probably rat-infested thigh-high grass to search for them. In fact, I didn't even want to go anywhere near my shoes again. Instead, I tucked the packets into my hoodie pocket, praying that would be a good enough place to keep it safe.

I was tempted to turn around and quick-step it out of there, but with the one glimpse of light from my phone, I'd caught sight of the greenhouse door, less than three feet in front of me.

I sucked in a deep breath, flicked on my flashlight app for another quick second, and then tiptoed forward. The area in front of the door had been cleared of long grass, and a cleared path led to the back door of the farmhouse, which made sense if the Albrights came in and out to water daily. It took all of my mental strength to put all vermin out of my mind, feel for the padlock on the door, and kneel in front of it so I could get a closer look.

I flicked on my flashlight app again and found it was a simple padlock. That's what I was hoping for. I wouldn't have had a clue where to start if it had been a combination or dial lock of some kind, but back when I helped Cooper research his novels, I'd had to "help" his main character, Marty Sims, pick more than a few simple padlocks. I'd never done it myself, but I'd typed the words about nestling a tension wrench into the top part of the lock and pushing the pins in one by one so many times, it felt like it should be a simple process.

I felt around for my paperclip in the dark, hoping it would work to emulate a tension wrench. Within seconds, I realized one thing: Marty Sims had a lot more skill as a detective than Mallory Beck did. The paperclip didn't have enough tension to move anything within the lock. I grabbed for my tiny flathead screwdriver.

I turned on my flashlight app and held my phone's empty penholder between my teeth so I could get a better look. Maybe this wasn't a job that could be done by a novice lock picker in the dark, after all.

But I was here now. I had to at least try.

The small screwdriver had enough strength that I could tell right away it was going to be more useful than the paperclip. Once I had it fed into the top part of the lock and pulled to the left, which was the direction I was quite sure it should turn, I reached back into my pocket for the paperclip.

Now that I had the lock mechanism held with some tension, I could actually feel the pins on the other end of my paperclip. It wasn't exactly a cinch to push them down, and it was definitely like riding a unicycle through a labyrinth while curling my hair to press them all at once, but I gave it all of my focus and tried again and again until finally I felt a click and the lock turned!

I was so excited, I almost let out a yelp. But just as I turned the lock fully to the other side to unhook it from the greenhouse's latch, my phone died and everything went dark.

"Shoot," I whispered aloud to the air around me. "Now what?"

"Now..." a deep male voice said from behind me, "you'll get up off the ground and tell me what you're doing breaking into my greenhouse."

Chapter Nineteen

MY KNEES AND HANDS shook as I rose to my feet. Brock Albright was intimidating at the best of times, but now, in the dead of night, he seemed like the Grim Reaper. He shone a flashlight in my face as I turned, blinding me.

"I—I'm sorry," I said. There was no avoiding or explaining away what I might have been doing, breaking and entering into his greenhouse in the dead of night.

Sounds emanated from the greenhouse now. Chattering sounds. Rustling. Screeching. There was more than one animal in there.

"You can tell it to the police," Brock said, roughly grabbing me by the arm.

My eyes had only just started to adjust to the light when Brock yanked me toward the back door of his house. He led me first through a small shed that smelled of vinegar and chemicals. The counters on either side were littered with metal netting, latches, and other building supplies, but I got a flash of one out-of-place object as we passed quickly through the shed and into the house: a bright yellow Nerf dart!

As he hauled me in through the back door, Brock yelled, "Katrina, call the police! We have an intruder."

He pushed me into a tiny kitchen, barely big enough for the two of us, but apparently, this was as far as he planned to take me. A stove light dimly lit a kitchen covered in peeling wallpaper that appeared to be at least three decades old. Brock wore yellow plaid pajama pants and a white T-shirt. His hair was mussed. I had definitely gotten him out of bed. I figured he must have heard me when I stepped on the dead rat and couldn't completely quell my scream.

A moment later, Katrina Albright swept into the small kitchen, and now there truly wasn't room for another person. Brock had me backed up against the stove, while he stood at the counter across from me. Katrina, in her baggy beige nightdress, widened her eyes at me and then looked at her feet when she turned to her husband and murmured, "I'm sorry."

She was sorry for having invited me in two days ago. I had gotten sweet Katrina Albright in trouble with her husband.

Then again, what was a Nerf dart doing in their shed? I'd be willing to bet if I'd had another moment to look around, I'd find more evidence, maybe needle-like darts. For all I knew, these two could've been in it together.

Katrina Albright turned and lifted a phone receiver from the wall. I had seen those kinds of phones in museums before, and I watched in awe as she ran a finger in a circle all the way from the 9 to the top and let the rotary dial click back into its place.

I snapped out of my daze when she dialed the second 1. She really was calling the police on me, which was a good thing, I told myself, even if the only two officers were out of reach for the evening. I'd rather spend the night in jail than with these crazy people.

Katrina started murmuring quietly into the phone. She gave the address of their farmhouse.

"I lost a necklace," I blurted the second the idea came to me. "I thought it might have fallen off in your grass somewhere." It was out of my mouth before I realized that wouldn't explain me trying to break into their greenhouse or even forcing my way into their backyard.

Brock let out a single bitter laugh. "And you didn't think to ask, perhaps when you were here during the daytime?" He laughed again.

"And would you have let me look for it?" I crossed my arms, trying hard to adopt some of Amber's confidence.

Brock raised his eyebrows. Then he grabbed me roughly by the arm again and pulled me out the back door the way we had come. This time, I was a little less in shock and a little more prepared. My eyes darted to every nook and cranny of his small shed as we passed through it.

It was too much to scan in a short amount of time, but as we moved outdoors, I caught sight of scattered straw on the ground. What looked like cat litter strewn on a work shelf. Spray bottles. And that bright yellow dart.

I sucked in a breath as we hit the night air. It still wasn't undeniable proof, but I felt it in my gut. Brock Albright had to be the murderer.

I just somehow had to find undeniable proof before the police arrived.

Brock eyed me as he pocketed the small padlock I had picked, as though I might steal it, and yanked open the sturdy greenhouse door. "Is this what you were looking for?" He shone his flashlight around the greenhouse, lined down one side with garden beds, the wood and soil barely visible for all the green foliage. Then he flipped a loud switch, and a series of what looked like grow lights illuminated one by one along the entire length of the greenhouse. I wondered why he didn't use clear plastic and harness the light from the sun like normal greenhouses.

But then a squeal from the other side of the greenhouse took my attention, and then rustling and more squeals, and I looked to that side to see rows of wire cages, at least a dozen of them, each one housing an individual rat.

I stepped back toward the door, but Brock blocked my path. "Oh, no. You're not going anywhere." He let out a low chuckle.

At least the police would be here soon. I surveyed the rat cages— certainly glad these ones were housed, not like the dead one outside. Halfway along was another worktable, this one metal, and it was covered in test tubes, test tube trays, small clear plastic baggies, and a large plastic bag that appeared to contain dried plants of some kind. My mind went first to marijuana, but only for a second. Then it went to the sciadotenia toxifera plant I had googled earlier. There were also plenty of baggies already packed with the green, dried substance and marked with stickers and names. Was he actually selling lethal plants to other people? The lady in the red car hadn't looked to me like someone out purchasing a murder weapon, but then again, would I think that of anyone?

The rats were all awake now and racing around in their cages. They were hard to turn my back on, but I had to scan the other sides of the greenhouse for the South African plant.

"Wow," I said, trying to buy time to gather as much intel as I could. "You have a real green thumb." Many of the plants were just large leafy ones, but a strain right near the door had smaller leaves and yellow berries. "Do you know where I can buy these sorts of plants or what they're called?"

One glance at Brock's hardened jaw, and I doubted he was going to answer. "Let's cut the ruse, shall we?" He gave me a small shove deeper into the greenhouse, followed me all the way in, and shut the door behind us. The rats went crazy with squealing. Him showing off his greenhouse to me definitely felt more eerie than prideful. "You're here because you think I killed Candi Banks." He said it in such a conversational tone, I would swear we were discussing garden tools or mundane yard work.

I sucked in a breath and let it out slowly before answering. The police were on their way, there was no stopping that. Maybe honesty really was the best approach in talking any new information out of Brock Albright before they arrived. I'd have to let the police cuff me and haul me out in the back of a police cruiser. Then I could tell them to get a hold of Alex, tell him everything I'd discovered.

"Did you?" I asked, trying to match his calmness, but my voice squeaked as high as one of the rats on the second word.

In way of an answer, Brock moved over to one of the nearby plant beds. He ran a hand along the soil under some large green leaves with red-tinged veins. His hand emerged with what looked like a tiny silver spigot, like the kind used to extract maple syrup from maple trees, but much smaller.

"We have plants from all over the world in here, Mallory," he said, and I admit, I was surprised he remembered my name. Although, come to think of it, even when I first brought over the casserole, he had acted as though they seldom had people inside their house. "These plants require constant monitoring of humidity and soil acidity. Some of them are even poisonous." He paused, as if for added effect. "We don't normally allow any outside visitors inside the greenhouse." He explained this as though he were doing me a favor by holding me hostage until the police came.

But there was the Nerf dart and what looked like the same plant Candi and Pastor Jeff were poisoned with. There was a worktable with test tubes. I knew there had to be needle-like darts somewhere on there as well.

He had never wanted his son to marry Candi, even though David had been determined to do so, so he had motive.

"Except for me?" I asked it as a question, wondering if he'd explain why I was given an honor that even his only precious son wasn't.

"Except for you." Brock nodded and smiled. Again, his tone gave me an eerie feeling that made my stomach drop out from within me. He took the tiny silver spigot, moved a step toward the door, lifted some of the small leaves around the yellow berries, and dug the spigot into the stem of the plant, right near the soil.

Was he actually bragging to me about how he'd accomplished a cold-blooded murder while the police were on their way? I glanced toward the door, straining to hear police sirens, but they must not have been close enough yet. If I tried to run, he'd certainly make it to the door before me.

"This one is called a sciacentaria toxifera," he told me conversationally as he pulled the spigot away from the plant and held it up to eye level, so both he and I could see the drops of orange liquid sitting in the groove of it. "African descent," he went on. "The root juices are highly poisonous to humans." He glanced over at me with an easy smile that made my stomach drop even further. "The poison is rare, so it often gets mistaken for strychnine." He took a step toward me.

Strychnine—the poison that was initially suspected to be in Candi's bloodstream.

"Is that what you used to kill Candi?" My throat was parched, so my question came out quieter than I meant it.

One side of his lip turned up as he told me, "The girl wouldn't leave David alone. I forbid him to see her, and still, she kept begging him to sneak out to meet her. She'd come by at all hours of the night. It's why we had the surveillance cameras installed around the property."

It hadn't been my reaction to the rat that had given me away after all. At least not entirely. But I couldn't get over the fact that Brock Albright had just admitted his guilt, and while the police were about to arrive.

"So you had to kill her?" I asked as I took a step backward in the small aisle way between the row of poisonous plants and the row of rats, not really wanting to get closer to either.

He mimicked my move. "I tried threatening her. I tried threatening him. But she was bound and determined to steal our son from us. For a minute there, I thought that with the double-booking of the park, the wedding might fall apart on its own and then everything would be fine. But then my son flashed a shiny key at me and told me that either way, he'd already moved his stuff into a house Mr. Banks had provided for him and their daughter and he wouldn't be back. I had to take care of her. I had to." He tilted his head at me, as though pleading for my understanding.

But I didn't understand. This was *murder*.

"The truth is, that church treasurer killed her." He said this as though this genuinely uplifted his spirits. "I had no idea about her bee allergy. If not for Mr. Offenbach's administration of the epinephrine, she likely would have made it to the hospital in time for them to help her." He took a breath and sighed it out. "My part was small. I just had to get the toxin into her from a distance. But there were plenty of shrubs and trees around that park to hide behind." He actually chuckled as he reminisced. "Of course, it was only my good fortune that the park had been double-booked and that Candi loved to argue. It gave me just the distraction I needed."

His good fortune? Sure. He sure didn't seem broken up that the EpiPen had sped up Candi's death. "The police should be here soon," I reminded him because the way he held the spigot, along with his creepy smile, felt like a threat.

But my words only made him laugh. "Oh, no. They won't be, my dear," he told me. "That old phone in the kitchen? It hasn't worked in years."

My knees buckled, and the next thing I knew, I fell onto the dirt beneath me.

With a renewed fierceness and confidence in his eyes, Brock Albright and his poison-filled spigot loomed above my head.

Chapter Twenty

THE MAN WITH THE POISON looked so calm and almost cheery, it seemed surreal when suddenly his hand reached out and he pushed me the rest of the way down so I fell face-first on the dirt floor of the greenhouse. It felt as though it took me hours—days—to react, but when I finally attempted to push myself up, his foot was already on my back, forcing me down.

"You won't get away with this!" I told him when I could find my voice.

My mind raced to Alex, who I told I was waiting for his call to discuss coming to the Albright farm. What were the chances he would guess that I had rushed out here on my own? He probably just figured I'd gone to bed for the night, and that was why I hadn't answered my phone. He had planned to drop by my house first thing in the morning. But morning was still hours away.

"Oh, sure I will," Brock told me. I felt a prick in the middle of my back. "In fact, I already have."

A second later, the pressure lifted from my back and I could move, but I didn't have time to worry about Brock. My arms flailed wildly to get at my back because one thing was clear to me: He had just poisoned me with the same type of needle-like dart he'd used on Candi Banks. The only difference was, at this close range, the dart in me hadn't come from a toy gun. Brock had simply dipped it in poison and then pressed it into my skin, like a hot knife through butter.

He knew exactly where to insert it so I wouldn't be able to reach it. I started to push myself up, but I didn't get very far. Suddenly, I wasn't concerned at all about my back or the needle because the toxin hit my bloodstream and I gasped for a breath. My hands flew to my throat, shocked at how fast the poison was affecting me.

"Don't fight it," Brock said in the same smooth voice he'd been using ever since he brought me into his greenhouse/lab.

My world had been turned on its head in the last thirty seconds and focusing on anything at all around me was getting more and more difficult.

His voice wobbled in my head when he added, "If I had some epinephrine on hand, I'd give it to you. It would make the whole process go a lot faster. But don't worry. It'll still be over within a matter of minutes. I know it's probably pointless to tell you this…" He let out a low chuckle that seemed completely out of place in this moment. "But struggling against the process will only make it more painful."

I didn't know whether he was lying or not. Perhaps he wanted me to stop struggling so the poison would have a chance to move seamlessly through my veins. Whatever the case, I did what he said. Somehow, in the depths of my mind, I knew I needed to conserve my energy. I also needed to stop reacting for a few seconds and think.

I kept my hands at my neck, as though that would somehow protect my lungs from the poison that had already infiltrated them, but the second I stopped struggling, Brock turned me over onto my back. I flopped like a rag doll and didn't fight him as he pawed at my hoodie. A second later, my keys jangled in his hand. My car! Hunch! I was doing everything in my power to keep my focus, conserve my energy, and come up with any kind of a plan that could save my life.

"Heh, heh, heh." Brock held a rectangular object right in front of my face, as if teasing me with it. "We wouldn't want you to have this, now would we?"

I blinked until it came into focus. My phone!

I swatted to grab for it. Brock was much quicker than me, though. He stood and pulled it away in plenty of time. Only a second later, I clued in enough to remember it was dead, anyway. It wasn't going to help me. But I couldn't help tracing the form of it with my eyes.

Just before he pocketed my phone, my eyes landed on the little leather pen loop.

My life-saving solution clicked into place in my mind like a bullet in a gun chamber. The revelation made me momentarily forget that my lungs were paralyzed and my mouth attempted to gasp for another breath. My inability to process the breath made my whole body writhe in pain as I struggled against my whole respiratory system.

"I told you," Brock said, backing toward the door with my phone and my keys in his pocket. "Just let it happen. I'll be back when it's over."

For once, Brock's tone, as much as I could concentrate on it, had changed to something less comfortable. *The coward*, I thought. He was man enough to poison me, but he wasn't man enough to stand around and watch me die?

But the second the door closed behind him, I remembered: I had a plan.

My hand immediately fumbled from my neck down to my right hoodie pocket. But I reached inside, fumbled around, and all I found was the screwdriver, paperclip, and hair clip. Frantically, I tried the other pocket. I hadn't been able to take a breath in what felt like an hour, and black spots filled my vision, but at least I still had feeling in my fingertips.

But the antidote packets weren't in there either!

Had they fallen out of my pocket outside? I slapped every area of my chest and stomach, willing them to appear. What if they'd fallen out when Brock had grabbed my phone?

I pawed the dirt around me and, sure enough, felt one packet, and then the other one, buried half under my side.

I didn't have the energy or the vision to look around to see if Brock had actually left. I tried to steady my hand as I ripped at the top of the packet. The black spots were making me dizzy, and I hoped I wasn't spilling it everywhere.

I'd pulled the packet to my mouth, tipped it back, but my mouth was numb, and I couldn't tell if the antidote made it to my mouth. I recalled what Emily Hawthorne had told me—about Pastor Jeff having been instructed to put it under his tongue to act faster, but I had no idea how to work my tongue anymore. I ripped open the other packet, dumped it into my mouth, and hoped some of it would by chance find its way under my tongue.

And then everything went black.

Chapter Twenty-one

MY FIRST BREATH FELT like a knife through my ribs, and I had to wonder if babies felt this kind of pain taking their first breath coming out of the womb. I gripped my chest and gulped for more oxygen. And then more.

My entire body felt achy and sore, but I blinked up and remembered where I was, on the floor of the Albright's greenhouse. And I could see. I could *breathe*.

There was no time for rejoicing. Brock Albright would be back to bury me or throw me into the river or whatever he planned to do with my dead body, but I didn't intend to be here. I needed to get to the police.

Sitting up took about as much effort as swimming the Atlantic with a tractor-trailer on my back. I turned onto my side. Rested. Pulled up a leg. Took another rest. Got my hands beneath me just in time for my next break. With each motion, I was convinced Brock Albright would return before I could even get myself up off the ground. But I focused and kept working at it anyway, one baby step at a time.

When I'd made it to my hands and knees, that seemed good enough. Why did humans have to walk on two legs anyway? This was much more stable. It certainly took less effort.

I moved on all fours toward the greenhouse door like an overweight hog that hadn't been out of his pen in a year. My muscles shook and ached with the effort of each step. I didn't know if the grow lamps in here were giving off heat or if it was just my own body breaking into a feverish sweat. The rats were no longer squealing, but I felt their eyes on me, like they were waiting for me to keel over so they could break out and feed on me. It felt like I weighed a literal tonne. When I finally made it to the door, I nudged it with my forehead.

It didn't budge.

I used all my effort to reach up and see if there was a knob of some kind to turn, but there was nothing. I pushed harder, this time with both hands and all my weight.

But the door clacked against something on the other side, and in my mind's eye, I could see exactly what was stopping the motion: the padlock I'd picked what felt like hours ago.

I fell back onto my rear, and if I'd had the energy, I would've cried. All this work, all this *hope*, and I was going to die anyway! How could that be possible?

I gazed around at probably fifty feet of green foliage on one side and two dozen beady eyes on the other. I suspected Brock did work some sort of a drug operation here—one he had kept secret from his son. While David was out hawking the vegetables from their overgrown yard at a farmer's market, likely to just keep him out of the way, his dad was making the real money—harvesting some sort of plant products to sell to local high school students. I didn't see any marijuana plants, so Brock likely dealt in some sort of more exotic drugs.

I supposed this wasn't the worst place to die. At least it was beautiful and earthy. The multitude of shades of green reminded me of Alex, of his eyes. If only Alex were here. I sighed. If only I'd called him back while I still had a phone and some battery life. But as I surveyed the magnificent but deadly plants in front of me, it was Cooper's voice I clearly heard in my head.

Start with what you have.

It's what Cooper always used to say to himself when stuck at some point in one of his mysteries. Hunch would pace alongside him, and before long, he'd stop mid-step, snap his fingers, and smile like the sun had illuminated his mouth.

I looked around again and argued out loud to Cooper. "But what do I have, except a whole lot of plants, most of them probably poisonous, and a dozen rats? Should I poison myself again, huh? Should I let the rats loose to start feeding on my arms and legs?" My voice came out angrier than I expected. It took me aback. Was I angry at *Cooper* that I'd gotten myself into this situation?

But before I'd even asked myself that question, I knew the answer. No. I was only angry because Cooper had left me. I sighed to myself again. He couldn't have helped that any more than I could have.

In a show of some sort of forgiveness or apology to Cooper's spirit, I dug in my hoodie pockets again, even though I knew my phone and keys were gone. I only had a tiny screwdriver, a hair clip, and a paperclip.

Start with what you have.

I looked at the greenhouse door and sighed. Unfortunately, the padlock was on the *outside* of the metal door, so these wouldn't do me much good. I dropped them onto the dirt beside me and had a momentary vision of trying to dig my way out of here using my tiny screwdriver.

"That should take, what, about a year?" I asked out loud and then laughed humourlessly. My laugh turned into a sob. I choked and muttered, "Please, God," as though I could actually count on Him to get me out of this.

But then, as though God or Cooper or *someone* up there was answering my question, a gust of wind rustled the black plastic greenhouse covering.

I blinked. And then blinked again, waiting for a slow-dawning realization to make it into my tired brain.

Plastic. Huh. Maybe I couldn't dig myself out through the dirt floor of the greenhouse, but what if I could dig my way out through the plastic?

The thought had barely formed and I was already lying on the ground, but this time not for a rest. I rolled under the closest plant bed, right up to the edge of the greenhouse, reached for the tiny screwdriver, and punctured it into the plastic.

I guess I expected it to let out a sigh of air, like a balloon slowly popping, but the screwdriver puncturing the plastic was much more innocuous. It didn't matter how it felt,

I decided quickly, puncturing another dozen holes around it. It would feel good enough to get out of here and be free.

But it seemed to be three layers of the heavyweight plastic. At this rate, it would take me all night to puncture enough holes through the plastic to even get my arm through.

I rolled out and sat up again, looking around. The tiny bit of success had been enough to fill me with a little extra hope and energy. My eyes roamed the rat cages—and for a second, I wondered if I could somehow convince them that rather than gnawing on me, they might enjoy a meal of black plastic—but then landed on the metal worktable.

The test tubes. Were they glass? They had to be.

I crawled forward and heaved myself up by the bed of the heavyset table. Sure enough, the empty test tubes were made of glass. They were less than an inch around, and there had to be at least twenty of them, but I only needed one. Sharp broken glass would cut plastic a lot easier than a tiny screwdriver would.

The thick plastic took a lot of puncturing and slicing before I could even force an arm through it, and it had as many holes as a screen door by the time I could force my feet and then the rest of my body through. I had effectively ruined about three feet of the Albright's precious greenhouse/lab, and I had to admit, even though it wasn't enough, it still felt pretty satisfying.

Once I had my entire body outside, I took eight or nine deep breaths of the cool night air before I had the energy to move.

"Thank you," I whispered into the night air. I didn't know if I was saying the words to God. But I couldn't say for sure that I wasn't.

Now what? Brock would certainly be coming back for me soon. I didn't have the energy to fight him or even his wife off in my current condition.

Then again, I didn't have car keys or a phone. I hadn't had the strength to pull myself to my feet yet, so how did I expect to walk half a mile down the road to my car? Even if I got there, was teaching Hunch how to hit the unlock button or teaching myself how to hotwire a car a possibility? No and no. So that left the nearest farm, which was even farther.

But it was my only choice, I quickly decided. And regardless of any possible vermin, dead or alive, I figured I had a better chance of making it to a neighboring farm on all fours than I did on two feet.

I took one grueling hog-like step after another around the front of the greenhouse, past the door, past the shed that led to the farmhouse, and into the long grass. It wasn't as though I loved dead rats, so I navigated around the one I knew was there, which kept me closer to the greenhouse, rather than the farmhouse. Even though the greenhouse was lit up like the light of day on the inside, only small cracks of light shone through to the outside. Still, it was easier to see than it had been on my way in, and despite my exhaustion, I quickly made it past the edge of the farmhouse.

As I turned the corner, new lights illuminated my way through the farmhouse windows. The Albrights were clearly still awake inside, probably discussing what to do with my dead body, but they weren't in view through any windows, so I kept low, crawling knee after hand, hand after knee until I reached the gate of the high fence.

Using all my might, I pulled myself up to reach for the handle.

When the gate didn't immediately move, for a second, I thought Brock had found and removed Amber's gum. But it turned out it was only my lack of strength holding me back.

I made it all the way past their old truck before I started to breathe a little easier. I looked both ways down the long farm road, only illuminated by the moonlight. That one barn light down past my car was my only beacon of hope. Who knew how far the next farmhouse would be, and could I even make it that far? What if the folks who lived there were friends with the Albrights and called them instead of the cops?

Too many unanswerable questions.

Even though the moonlight seemed at its brightest, I couldn't even make out the shape of my car from here. Part of me wondered if my eyes and brain still weren't working correctly after passing out from lack of oxygen. I swore I could even see black shadows moving on the street in front of me.

I sighed away my questions and confusion and went to take another slow knee-and-hand step toward the pavement, figuring I had to try for the nearest farm. But that's when Brock's voice stopped me.

"How are you still alive?" He sounded astonished as his black form came into focus in front of me on the road.

I groaned inwardly. Even if I had the energy to explain, the last thing I wanted to do was to tip him off that the police had an antidote to his poison before I died.

He jangled some keys, and in an instant, it became clear to me why he was coming from down the road and why I couldn't see my Prius. He had been concealing it, apparently. When he killed me, there would be nothing to lead the police to my being here.

I squinted my eyes shut and then opened them, wondering, if I pooled every single resource inside my body, how far I would be able to stumble away from this crazy man. Could I lift my leg enough to try and kick him in the groin? I sucked in my breath, ready to try.

But as I wobbled to my feet, Brock was quick to grab both of my arms and hold them together in a grip I didn't have a hope of fighting. I already knew he would take me back to his greenhouse/lab and poison me again.

And this time I had no antidote to fight it.

Chapter Twenty-two

I LOOKED UP AT BROCK, but his eyes weren't on me. They were down the farm road. When I followed his gaze, I saw two bright lights coming straight toward us.

These weren't the bright lights of the afterlife I was expecting either. These were the lights of a car barreling full-speed ahead.

Brock yanked me toward the roadside, but the car picked up speed and skidded to a stop at an angle, only ten feet away from the Albright's driveway where Brock had now pulled me. Before he could get any farther, two car doors slammed behind us, and a deep, authoritative voice said, "This is the police! Brock Albright, get your hands in the air!"

I had never been so happy to hear Detective Reinhart's voice. Brock hesitated, but then let me go and raised his hands.

I took a step forward, away from him, but wobbled on my feet. "He did it!" I panted my words out as loudly as I could as I pointed back over my shoulder. "He murdered Candi Banks!"

It was all the energy I had left. I started to collapse forward, and Alex rushed forward from the other side of the car to catch me.

Chapter Twenty-three

I WOKE UP IN THE back of an ambulance with a large oxygen mask covering the lower half of my face.

"Alex?" I said, trying to pull myself into a sitting position, but I'd been strapped to a gurney. The back doors of the ambulance were wide open, and I could see miles of farmland, now lit up by giant work lights, and the tiny distant light of the neighbor's barn.

A paramedic turned to me from within the ambulance. "Whoa, whoa.

You're okay, ma'am. Just relax." He was the same paramedic who had treated me after my near-drowning while tracking down the murderer of Dan Montrose. I wondered if this paramedic thought I just enjoyed this kind of life-threatening adrenaline rush. I wondered if we should be past him calling me "ma'am" by now.

"Alex Martinez?" I asked.

My voice sounded muffled through the oxygen mask, but he must have heard me because he said, "Officer Martinez will check in with you at the hospital. He had to arrange to get some arrests to the station first."

"Arrests?" My hope soared, but the paramedic seemed to realize he'd said too much and patted my shoulder.

"Don't you worry about that. Just get some rest."

I didn't see Alex until I had been poked and prodded a million times at the hospital. Thankfully, I remembered the name of Dr. Khumalo, the doctor who had treated Pastor Jeff, and I asked for him as soon as the paramedics wheeled me through the emergency entrance.

It took some time for the hospital staff to track him down, but as soon as he walked into the ER room they'd parked me in, I started spewing information at him.

"I was injected with the same type of toxin as Pastor Jeff Hawthorne. I had the H2-blocker/antacid antidote with me. I swallowed some, and I could breathe again, but my lungs are still working so hard and I'm so tired." I let out a wheeze of air to punctuate the statement.

Dr. Khumalo nodded with his forehead creased. Then he rattled off a slew of instructions to nearby nurses:

eight cc's of this, five of that. I was just so tired. I couldn't concentrate on any of it.

Thankfully, whatever Dr. Khumalo prescribed, it allowed me to sleep.

The next time I awoke, I was greeted with a beautiful combination of greens. But these weren't from surrounding poisonous plants that might kill me. These were Alex's warm and worried eyes.

"Did you arrest them?" I asked. My voice croaked, but the oxygen mask had been removed. I must at least be breathing properly on my own now.

"Well, good morning to you, too," he said, smiling with one side of his mouth in a way that made him look a lot like he had in seventh grade. Judging by the dim light around the window curtains, it must have been really early. "And, yes, the Albrights are behind bars. Our forensic scientists have already been able to verify the poisonous species of plants that were responsible for Candi Banks' death."

"There's a shed behind the farmhouse, too," I told him. "You'll find at least one Nerf bullet inside. There's probably more evidence, but I didn't get a chance to look around much."

"Not much?" Alex raised his eyebrows at me. "Just enough to almost get yourself killed. Again," he added. He pulled out a notebook and jotted down everything I told him.

"Did you see his whole drug operation? Was he selling lethal dried plants to other people?" If this was the case, there could be a lot more danger out there.

But Alex shook his head. "We found the setup, yes, but when Steve questioned Brock Albright, he admitted to selling a plant substance that mimics OxyContin. He had recently been fired from Brem Chemical Plant in Martinsburg for suspicion of stealing equipment. Apparently, he had tried to find out about getting FDA approval, but he was out of work and didn't have time or money for the years' long process." Alex shook his head. "I actually got the impression the guy had good intentions—to provide an alternative to a dangerous drug. But where he's going, he won't be supplying anyone for a good long while, with or without FDA approval."

"I guess Amber's brother had it a little off the mark when he thought the Albrights were Honeysuckle Grove's biggest drug dealers," I said.

Alex nodded. "We haven't found a connection to the toy gun that fired any Nerf bullets and needles yet. Our forensics team said it's only available in the UK."

"Katrina Albright's mother sent toys from England each year!" It felt a little like I had the right answer on Jeopardy. Even though the case was solved, more puzzle pieces fitting into place felt very satisfying. Alex made a note of this, too.

"When you're feeling better, I can't wait for you to tell me why you thought it was a good idea to sneak around a murderer's backyard in the middle of the night."

That smile was fighting at the sides of his lips again, and I knew Alex wasn't angry with me. Just worried. And once I explained I'd done it for him—if things had worked out how I had wanted them to, he would've been able to go back to Detective Reinhart and Captain Corbett with a solid case, one only he could take credit for—I knew he'd understand.

"For now, though," he told me, "you'd just better take a few deep breaths and help me get your story straight about why you might have had a reason to be trespassing on the Albright farm because Reinhart and Corbett are on their way in to talk to you."

Chapter Twenty-four

WHEN I WOKE UP the next time, Detective Reinhart and Captain Corbett loomed above me in their police uniforms. I had no idea how much time had passed since Alex had been by my side, but it looked brighter outside my hospital room window. Even though Alex had been dressed equally formally when he had been here earlier, his appearance had felt a whole lot friendlier. These two men, with their grim faces, looked like they were out for somebody's blood.

Probably mine.

But I took a deep breath—it was getting easier and easier to do that—and said, "Good morning, gentlemen. What can I do for you?"

"We have some questions for you about the incident at the Albright farm last night," Captain Corbett said. Despite his gruff early-morning voice, his authoritative Texan twang still rang through.

"If you're up to it," Detective Reinhart added. He offered a small smile, which earned him a glare from his superior.

"Will Officer Martinez be joining us?" I asked. I already knew he hadn't been invited for this interview, but it didn't mean I wouldn't try.

"Officer Martinez has other obligations within the hospital this morning," Captain Corbett told me. I wished the two men in my room would sit down. They felt intimidating and stress-inducing looming over me. Then again, that was probably their intention. At least Captain Corbett's. "But don't worry, I think Detective Reinhart and I can handle it."

His sarcasm wasn't lost on me, and it was all I could do not to act sarcastic right back and mention how inappropriate his tone was while talking to a victim who had almost died at the hands of a murderer that, as of last night, he hadn't yet caught.

But while Alex and I had discussed my presence at the Albrights' earlier, I had thought this through and had come up with a plan. I opened my mouth to say, "You know, I'd really feel much more comfortable if Officer Martinez was here. He was just so calm and compassionate when I collapsed at the Albright farm." I used my sweetest, most innocent voice to add, "After everything I've been through, I'd just feel better." I sucked in my lips to refrain from spewing all the other things I wanted to say to Alex's bossy, unreasonable captain.

"Officer Martinez is not officially working this case."

I kept my wide eyes right on the police captain. "Well, maybe he should be. After all he's done on this case, should he not at least be in the room to verify any details?" I folded my arms across my chest and waited him out.

He twisted his lips to the side and, after a long pause, offered a single nod to Detective Reinhart— apparently a dismissal. As the detective left the room, he shot me a look with raised eyebrows that I swear was admiration. As soon as the door shut behind him, another miracle happened: Captain Corbett sighed and decided to sit in the only other chair in my room.

"I can't wait to hear how it was y'all were involved so closely in another murder investigation, Mrs. *Beck*," he told me with a heavy accent on my last name. But it wasn't a direct question, and so I chose not to answer it.

Thankfully, Alex was still in the hospital, and it only took him mere minutes to appear in my stoically silent hospital room.

"Detective Reinhart said you wanted to see me," he said to his boss, and all I wanted in the world was for Alex to finally earn some respect from this man.

"Mrs. Beck has requested for you to sit in on this here interview," Corbett said. He sat back into his chair, relaxed, and had his arms spread out along the windowsill behind him in some sort of power pose. "So why don't you conduct this interview, Officer Martinez. We want to do whatever we can to make Mrs. Beck comfortable."

Again with the sarcasm. In that second, I made it my life's goal to stop focusing on the murderers of Honeysuckle Grove and focus my full attention on driving this bully out of town.

Alex cleared his throat, but we'd already had a practice run at this in the early morning. Alex had already told me, "Captain Corbett will want to ask you this...and then he'll ask you that..." And we had come up with a satisfactory answer for every single question.

I couldn't have asked for better fortune than to have Alex asking the questions. Now I'd be certain to be prepared for each one.

"I had delivered a casserole the day before on behalf of the church," I said to his first question, looking only at Alex. "Something seemed really suspicious about the locked greenhouse they had in the back. They were really evasive, and on my way out the back door, I'd gotten a glimpse of a Nerf bullet." So what if the timeline was off about what I was explaining? It was all still true.

"And you didn't think to call the police with this information rather than investigating yourself?" Corbett demanded.

"Oh, I wasn't out there investigating!" I said, following my preprepared script. "And I did call the police with that information."

"Detective Reinhart was planning to put in a request for a warrant the next morning, sir," Alex told his boss.

Captain Corbett scowled at him for a long moment and then turned back to me. "And so why was it that y'all were out there?"

"I had been getting ready for bed when I realized my locket was missing. It had been a gift from my late husband, and I simply couldn't go to sleep without it. I had the feeling it had fallen off somewhere in the Albrights' long grass when Katrina Albright had been escorting me out, and I simply had to go and find it."

"So y'all were there looking for a necklace in the middle of the night?" Corbett asked, disbelief clear in his every word.

I nodded with wide innocent eyes. So what if he didn't believe me? He couldn't prove I was lying, and it's what had to happen to get to the truth. If he wasn't willing to rework his division of labor on the force, perhaps civilians would have to be out there solving crimes on the regular.

But I held my tongue about all I wanted to say and simply told him, "I was being super quiet, and I found it." I held up my locket, which truly was precious to me. "But I guess somehow Mr. Albright heard me. He thought I was breaking into his greenhouse or something," I said as though that notion had never even crossed my mind.

Chapter Twenty-five

MY CELL PHONE HAD been retrieved from Brock Albright, but I couldn't charge it until I was released from the hospital and at home the next day. Because I'd swallowed the antidote so quickly after being poisoned, the poison's effects also hadn't been very long-lasting. Still, I went home with a handful of the little packets. When I finally booted up my phone, I had five missed texts and three missed calls, all from Amber.

Oh, no. I immediately felt sick and hoped she was okay.

It was two forty in the afternoon. She should have been just getting out of her last class. I was about to click her contact and dial when my phone rang in my hands.

"Hi!" I said before the name of the caller could register. I just assumed it would be her.

But after a long pause, a deep male voice replied. "Is this Mallory Beck?"

I cleared my throat and quelled my enthusiasm. "Yes, this is she."

"Steve Reinhart here," he said. "I didn't get a chance to speak to you again at the hospital before you were released."

I wondered if he was going to somehow swoop in and take credit for all of Alex's investigative work again. I leaned back into my couch and sighed, waiting for whatever kind of follow-up questions he was going to use to do that. "What can I help you with?" I said in a bland tone that lacked emotion.

"Well, first I wanted to check in on how you were feeling," he said, and his voice really did sound like it held some compassion.

But I couldn't help myself, the snide retort was on the tip of my tongue. "I'd feel a lot better if Alex could finally get some credit for an investigation and get officially promoted to detective work like he deserves."

Detective Reinhart's reply came quickly enough that I figured it had to be truthful. "Actually, I think that's in the works. I wondered if I could take you to dinner one night? We can chat more about it."

I furrowed my brow, wondering if he had talked this over with Alex. But my curiosity wouldn't seem to allow me to decline.

"Okay." I drew out the word.

"Great!" he said, peppier than I'd ever heard the detective. "Tomorrow night? I can pick you up at seven."

I had agreed and hung up the phone, eager to get to Amber, before it occurred to me that this sounded an awful lot like a date. To get my mind off that possibility, I quickly scrolled back to Amber's contact and dialed.

It took her five rings to answer, and when she did, all she said was, "Yeah?" in the same hard tone she'd used when she first tried to convince me her dad had been murdered.

"I'm so sorry I haven't returned your calls," I told her and figured the only thing that might make her soften was the truth. "I've been in the hospital."

A long pause followed. "Oh. How come?" she asked tentatively. She clearly hadn't expected me to have any excuse, let alone such a good one.

I shrugged, trying to get more comfortable without disturbing my sleeping cat. When I'd first sat down over half an hour ago, Hunch had taken all of about thirty seconds to haul his cast up onto my lap, curl up, and promptly fall asleep. After the Albrights had been arrested, Alex had located my car down the road and in the ditch, covered in brush. Hunch had still been locked inside, though I heard he'd clawed some damage into Brock Albright's arm during the process. The poor cat wouldn't admit to being shaken up any sooner than Amber would, but he probably hadn't slept a wink last night.

"I snuck around the Albrights', got caught, got poisoned with a toxic dart, almost died. You know, the usual." I clucked my tongue, and then because I knew Amber would need confirmation, I added, "Check the news. See what it says about the Albright farm."

I waited and could perfectly envision her on the other end of the phone, scrolling on her browser through news headlines. I knew she'd need to see it in black and white with her own eyes before she fully believed I wasn't just shrugging her off. Poor kid needed some sort of adult security in her life. If I had anything to say about it, I planned to give that to her.

"Huh," she said, which in Amber-language meant, *Okay, I'll at least half-believe you weren't ditching me.* "I called all day, and even called Alex again when I couldn't get a hold of you, but this time he didn't answer."

"Wait. Called Alex *again?*" I asked. When had she ever called Officer Alex Martinez?

"Yeah, I called him in the night, told him you said you always had your phone on, but it wasn't. I told him I was worried." I knew things like this were hard for Amber to admit, so it didn't surprise me when she rushed on with her words. "He told me everything would be fine, and he'd check up on you. Said he had to go right away, but then when you didn't answer again today, and even *he* hasn't returned my messages, I thought..."

She called Alex in the night? It hadn't occurred to me before how Alex had known to come and find me at the Albright farm, right when I'd needed him last night. It had been Amber's doing. She had called Alex. Alex had considered my message from earlier and knew me well enough to know that I'd gone running after another murder suspect.

He was going to get tired of saving me. They both were.

But for the moment, I had to reassure Amber I was okay and I wasn't about to desert her. How better to do that than with a cooking lesson?

"How's school been?" I asked, ready to pave the way back to her trusting me. Plus, I felt bad that I hadn't been around for her to decompress about her first day back.

She huffed out a breath. "As expected. Marcy Ralston whispered loud enough that she might as well have had a microphone about how my dad had been murdered. You know. The usual."

"Stupid Marcy Ralston," I said in solidarity, even though I didn't know the girl from anyone else in this town.

"Then all my teachers looked at me with tilted heads like they thought I might break down in tears right in front of them."

"The head tilt of pity. Sounds awful," I told her, knowing how much worse a pity-fest would feel to her than getting pushed or punched or outwardly teased. I had learned enough about Amber Montrose over the last few weeks to know that much. "Feel like cooking?" I asked. I felt bad for lifting Hunch off my lap, but all it took was a positive sigh out of Amber and I was heading for my car keys.

"I could cook," she told me, in way of an answer.

"Wait in front of your school. I'll pick you up."

As I got into the Prius, I envisioned freshly baked bread— something hearty and grainy that would take some serious effort for both of us to knead. Kneading was what we both needed right now. Kneading and trying to figure out if I'd accidentally agreed to date Detective Steve Reinhart.

"I'll be there in ten," I told her, already smelling fresh bread and freedom from all this stress in the air around me. "And I can't wait to tell you everything."

THE END

Up Next: Murder at the Town Hall...
A Mallory Beck Cozy Culinary Caper (Book 3)

An eye witness to a murder, a crush-worthy cop who needs her help, and a cat with a hunch. What could possibly go wrong?

Mallory Beck isn't in the habit of involving herself in local politics, but when she supports a new friend at a meeting to save the local library and the main speaker is found dead on the steps of the town hall, she finds herself deep in the heart of another murder investigation. Her cat, Hunch, who loves a good mystery is thrilled and, as usual, helps her discover a key clue.

Mallory's clever friend and long-ago crush, Alex, is on the case. He was recently promoted to detective within the Honeysuckle Grove Police Department, but when he's paired with a lackadaisical superior who continually botches investigations, Mallory and her famously delicious cooking come to the rescue.

After all, the easiest way to a suspect's truth might just be through their stomach.

Order Murder at the Town Hall now!

Join My Cozy Mystery Readers' Newsletter Today!

Would you like to be among the first to hear about new releases and sales, and receive special excerpts and behind-the-scene bonuses?

Sign up now to get your free copy of
Mystery of the Holiday Hustle
– A Mallory Beck Cozy Holiday Mystery.

You'll also get access to special epilogues to accompany this series—an exclusive bonus for newsletter subscribers. Sign up below and receive your free mystery:

https://www.subscribepage.com/mysteryreaders

Honest reviews help bring new books to the attention of other readers. If you enjoyed this book, I would be grateful if you would take five minutes to write a couple of sentences about it.

Here's where you can find Murder at the Church Picnic on Amazon:

https://www.amazon.com/gp/product/B08JRLTL3J

Thank you!

Turn the page to find a recipe from Mallory's Recipe Box...

Mallory's Potato Bacon Casserole

Crispy roasted potatoes, melted cheese, and plenty of crisp bacon—a perfect addition for a main dish or a side dish at your next potluck picnic! The secret to this potato recipe is a long roasting time and a good drizzling of bacon grease. The smoky bacon flavor is in every bite and the extra time in the oven leave the edges of each potato nice and crisp.

Ingredients:

1 pound bacon
2 extra large russet potatoes, peeled and chopped into ½" pieces
3 vitolette potatoes, peeled and chopped into ½" pieces
1 teaspoon kosher salt
3/4 teaspoon freshly ground black pepper

1 ½ cups shredded cheddar mixed with jack shredded cheeses
3 green onions sliced thin

Instructions:

BACON: Spread the bacon strips across a large rimmed baking sheet pan and place on the middle rack of a cold oven. Set the temperature to 400 degrees and time for 16 minutes. Check and cook for a couple more minutes if you like it crunchier. Remove it from the oven.

POTATOES: While the bacon cooks, peel and chop the potatoes (or if you prefer, rinse the potatoes and leave them unpeeled.) Transfer the bacon to a paper towel lined plate to drain. There should be 2-3 tablespoons of bacon grease left on the sheet pan. (If there is more, drain some off.) Put the potatoes on the pan and toss with tongs to thoroughly coat them in the bacon grease. Sprinkle with salt and pepper. Spread the potatoes out in a single layer and bake for 20 minutes, stir well and bake an additional 20 minutes. Stir again, making sure that none of the potatoes are sticking to the tray. Bake another 15 minutes.

Chop the bacon into small pieces.

Remove the potatoes from the oven, transfer to a large casserole dish, and sprinkle generously with shredded cheese and chopped bacon. Return the dish to the oven and bake an additional 2-3 minutes, until the cheese has melted. Top with sliced green onions just before serving.

Enjoy!

Acknowledgements

Thank you to my editor Angelika Offenwanger and copyeditor Sara Burgess. I feel incredibly fortunate to have your help and expertise on my side. Much appreciation to my son, Teddy Kewin, for great plot ideas whenever I'm stuck. Thanks to Ethan Heyde, the illustrator of my covers and to Steven Novak of Novak Illustrations for the beautiful design work on the cover.

Thanks to my beta readers and assistant plotters, who always add great insight and see things I've missed: Shelly Wielenga, Marj Nesbitt, Norma Zenky, Lisa Green, Donna Wollf, and Danielle Lucas. Your thoughts and suggestions have helped me immensely.

You are all proof that writing is not a solo sport.

Thank you all so much!

About Denise

Denise Jaden is a co-author of the Rosa Reed Mystery Series by Lee Strauss, the author of several critically-acclaimed young adult novels, as well as the author of several nonfiction books for writers, including the NaNoWriMo-popular guide Fast Fiction. Her new Mallory Beck Cozy Culinary Mystery Series will continue to launch throughout the year, and you can add the first book to your reading list on GoodReads right now. In her spare time, she homeschools her son (a budding filmmaker), acts in TV and movies, and dances with a Polynesian dance troupe. She lives just outside Vancouver, British Columbia, with her husband, son, and one very spoiled cat.

Sign up on Denise's website to receive bonus content as well as updates on her new Cozy Mystery Series. Find out more at www.denisejaden.com

Also by Denise Jaden

<u>The Mallory Beck Cozy Culinary Capers:</u>
Book 1 – Murder at Mile Marker 18
Book 2 – Murder at the Church Picnic
Book 3 – Murder at the Town Hall
Christmas Novella – Mystery of the Holiday Hustle

<u>Young Adult Fiction:</u>
Losing Faith
Never Enough
Foreign Exchange
A Christmas Kerril
The Living Out Loud Series

<u>Nonfiction for Writers:</u>
Writing with a Heavy Heart
Story Sparks
Fast Fiction